# CYRANO DE BERGERAC

# THE DRAMA LIBRARY

*General Editor:* EDWARD THOMPSON

# CYRANO DE BERGERAC

*by*

EDMOND ROSTAND

*Translated by*
BRIAN HOOKER

WILLIAM HEINEMANN LTD
GEORGE ALLEN & UNWIN LTD
LONDON

FIRST PUBLISHED IN ENGLAND
IN THE DRAMA LIBRARY 1953

*Published by*
WILLIAM HEINEMANN LTD.
99 Great Russell Street, London, W.C.1
*in association with*
GEORGE ALLEN & UNWIN LTD.
40 Museum Street, London, W.C.1

PRINTED IN GREAT BRITAIN FOR THE PUBLISHERS
BY MORRISON & GIBB LTD., LONDON AND EDINBURGH

It was to the soul of CYRANO that I intended to dedicate this poem.

But since that soul has been reborn in you, COQUELIN, it is to you that I dedicate it.

E. R.

# CONTENTS

The first four Acts take place in 1640; the fifth in 1655

# DRAMATIS PERSONÆ

---

| | |
|---|---|
| Cyrano de Bergerac | The Porter |
| Christian de Neuvillette | A Citizen |
| Comte de Guiche | His Son |
| Ragueneau | A Cut-Purse |
| Le Bret | A Spectator |
| Carbon de Castel-Jaloux | A Sentry |
| The Cadets | Bertrandou the Fifer |
| Lignière | A Capuchin |
| Vicomte de Valvert | Two Musicians |
| A Marquis | The Poets |
| Second Marquis | The Pastrycooks |
| Third Marquis | The Pages |
| Montfleury | Roxane |
| Bellerose | Her Duenna |
| Jodelet | Lise |
| Cuigy | The Orange Girl |
| Brissaille | Mother Marguérite de Jésus |
| A Meddler | Sister Marthe |
| A Musketeer | Sister Claire |
| Another Musketeer | An Actress |
| A Spanish Officer | A Comedienne |
| A Cavalier | The Flower Girl |

The Crowd, Citizens, Marquis, Musketeers, Thieves, Pastrycooks, Poets, Cadets of Gascoyne, Actors, Violinists, Pages, Children, Spanish Soldiers, Spectators, Intellectuals, Academicians, Nuns, etc.

# ACT I

## A PERFORMANCE AT THE
## HÔTEL DE BOURGOGNE

THE HALL OF THE HÔTEL DE BOURGOGNE in 1640. *A
sort of tennis court, arranged and decorated for theatrical
productions.*
*The hall is a long rectangle; we see it diagonally, in such a way
that one side of it forms the back scene, which begins at the first
entrance on the right and runs up to the last entrance on the left,
where it makes a right angle with the stage which is seen obliquely.
This stage is provided on either hand with benches placed along the
wings. The curtain is formed by two lengths of tapestry which can
be drawn apart. Above a harlequin cloak, the Royal Arms.
Broad steps lead from the stage down to the floor of the hall. On
either side of these steps, a place for the musicians. A row of
candles serving as footlights. Two tiers of galleries along the side
of the hall; the upper one divided into boxes.*
*There are no seats upon the floor, which is the actual stage of our
theatre; but toward the back of the hall, on the right, a few benches
are arranged; and underneath a stairway on the extreme right,
which leads up to the galleries, and of which only the lower portion
is visible, there is a sort of sideboard, decorated with little tapers,
vases of flowers, bottles and glasses, plates of cake, et cetera.*
*Farther along, toward the centre of our stage is the entrance to the
hall: a great double door which opens only slightly to admit the
audience. On one of the panels of this door, as also in other places
about the hall, and in particular just over the sideboard, are
playbills in red, upon which we may read the title* LA CLORISE.
*As the curtain rises, the hall is dimly lighted and still empty.
The chandeliers are lowered to the floor, in the middle of the hall,
ready for lighting.*

1

*Sound of voices outside the door. Then* A CAVALIER *enters abruptly.*

THE PORTER (*follows him*): Halloa there!—Fifteen sols!

THE CAVALIER:                                        I enter free.

THE PORTER: Why?

THE CAVALIER:      Soldier of the Household of the King!

THE PORTER (*turns to* SECOND CAVALIER *who has just entered*): You?

SECOND CAVALIER: I pay nothing.

THE PORTER:                          Why not?

SECOND CAVALIER:                                  Musketeer!

FIRST CAVALIER (*to the* SECOND):
      The play begins at two. Plenty of time—
      And here's the whole floor empty. Shall we try
      Our exercise?
      (*They fence with the foils which they have brought*)

A LACKEY (*enters*): Pst! . . . Flanquin! . . .

ANOTHER (*already on stage*):                What, Champagne?

FIRST LACKEY (*showing games which he takes out of his doublet*):
      Cards. Dice. Come on.                (*Sits on the floor*)

SECOND LACKEY:          Come on, old cock!

FIRST LACKEY (*takes from his pocket a bit of candle, lights it, sets it on the floor*)                        I have stolen
      A little of my master's fire.

A GUARDSMAN (*to a* FLOWER GIRL): How sweet
      Of you, to come before they light the hall!
      (*Puts his arm around her*)

FIRST CAVALIER (*receives a thrust of the foil*): A hit!

SECOND CAVALIER:                    A club!

THE GUARDSMAN (*pursuing* THE GIRL):      A kiss!

THE FLOWER GIRL (*pushing away from him*): They'll see us!—

THE GUARDSMAN (*draws her into a dark corner*): No danger!

A MAN (*sits on the floor, together with several others who have brought packages of food*):
      When we come early, we have time to eat.

A CITIZEN (*escorting his son, a boy of sixteen*): Sit here, my son.

FIRST LACKEY: Mark the Ace!

ANOTHER MAN (*draws a bottle from under his cloak and sits down with the others*): Here's the spot
For a jolly old sot to suck his Burgundy—
Here—in the house of the Burgundians!

THE CITIZEN (*to his son*):
Would you not think you were in some den of vice?
Drunkards—
(*In stepping back, one of the Cavaliers trips him up*)
Bullies!—
(*He falls between the lackeys*)
Gamblers!—

THE GUARDSMAN (*still struggling with the* FLOWER GIRL):
One kiss—

THE CITIZEN: Good God!—
(*Draws his son quickly away*)
Here!—And to think, my son, that in this hall
They play Rotrou!

THE BOY: Yes, Father—and Corneille!

THE PAGES (*dance in, holding hands and singing*):
Tra-la-la-la-la-la-la-la-la-lère . . .

THE PORTER: You pages there—no nonsense!

FIRST PAGE: Oh, monsieur!
Really! How could you?
(*To the* SECOND, *the moment the* PORTER *turns his back*):
Pst!—a bit of string?

SECOND PAGE (*shows fishline with hook*):
Yes—and a hook.

FIRST PAGE: Up in the gallery,
And fish for wigs!

A CUT-PURSE (*gathers around him several evil-looking young fellows*):
Now, then, you picaroons,
Perk up, and hear me mutter. Here's your bout—
Bustle around some cull, and bite his bung . . .

SECOND PAGE (*calls to other Pages already in the gallery*):
  Hey! Brought your pea-shooters?
THIRD PAGE (*from above*):                    And our peas, too!
      (*Blows, and showers them with peas*)
THE BOY: What is the play this afternoon?
THE CITIZEN:                         "Clorise."
THE BOY: Who wrote that?
THE CITIZEN:          Balthasar Baro. What a play! . . .
      (*He takes The Boy's arm and leads him upstage*)
THE CUT-PURSE (*to his pupils*):
  Lace now, on those long sleeves, you cut it off—
      (*Gesture with thumb and finger, as if using scissors*)
A SPECTATOR (*to another, pointing upward toward the gallery*):
  Ah, *Le Cid*!—Yes, the first night, I sat there—
THE CUT-PURSE: Watches—
      (*Gesture as of picking a pocket*)
THE CITIZEN (*coming down with his son*):
                    Great actors we shall see to-day—
THE CUT-PURSE: Handkerchiefs—
      (*Gesture of holding the pocket with left hand, and drawing
      out handkerchief with right*)
THE CITIZEN:                Montfleury—
A VOICE (*in the gallery*):          Lights! Light the lights!
THE CITIZEN: Bellerose, l'Epy, Beaupré, Jodelet—
A PAGE (*on the floor*): Here comes the Orange Girl.
THE ORANGE GIRL:                   Oranges, milk,
  Raspberry syrup, lemonade—
      (*Noise at the door*)
A FALSETTO VOICE (*outside*):              Make way,
  Brutes!
FIRST LACKEY: What, the Marquis—on the floor?
      (*The Marquis enter in a little group*)
SECOND LACKEY:                    Not long—
  Only a few moments; they'll go and sit
  On the stage presently.

FIRST MARQUIS (*seeing the hall half empty*):

How now! We enter
Like tradespeople—no crowding, no disturbance!—
No treading on the toes of citizens?
Oh fie! Oh fie!
(*He encounters two gentlemen who have already arrived*)
Cuigy! Brissaille!
(*Great embracings*)

CUIGY:                                             The faithful!
We are here before the candles.

FIRST MARQUIS:                            Ah, be still!
You put me in a temper.

SECOND MARQUIS:                   Console yourself,
Marquis—The lamplighter!

THE CROWD (*applauding the appearance of the lamplighter*):
Ah! . . .
(*A group gathers around the chandelier while he lights it. A
few people have already taken their places in the gallery.
LIGNIÈRE enters the hall, arm in arm with CHRISTIAN DE
NEUVILLETTE. LIGNIÈRE is a slightly dishevelled figure,
dissipated and yet distinguished looking. CHRISTIAN,
elegantly but rather unfashionably dressed, appears pre-
occupied and keeps looking up at the boxes*)

CUIGY:                                        Lignière!—

BRISSAILLE (*laughing*):
Still sober—at this hour?

LIGNIÈRE (*to* CHRISTIAN):          May I present you?
(CHRISTIAN *assents*)
Baron Christian de Neuvillette.
(*They salute*)

THE CROWD (*applauding as the lighted chandelier is hoisted into
place*):                          Ah!—

CUIGY (*aside to* BRISSAILLE, *looking at* CHRISTIAN): Rather
A fine head, is it not? The profile . . .

FIRST MARQUIS (*who has overheard*):          Peuh!

LIGNIÈRE (*presenting them to* CHRISTIAN):
    Messieurs de Cuigy . . . de Brissaille . . .
CHRISTIAN (*bows*):                  Enchanted!
FIRST MARQUIS (*to the second*):
              He is not ill-looking; possibly a shade
    Behind the fashion.
LIGNIÈRE (*to* CUIGY):        Monsieur is recently
    From the Touraine.
CHRISTIAN:             Yes, I have been in Paris
    Two or three weeks only. I join the Guards
    To-morrow.
FIRST MARQUIS (*watching the people who come into the boxes*):
              Look—Madame la Présidente
    Aubry!
THE ORANGE GIRL: Oranges, milk—
THE VIOLINS (*tuning up*): La . . . la . . .
CUIGY (*to* CHRISTIAN, *calling his attention to the increasing crowd*):             We have
    An audience to-day!
CHRISTIAN:        A brilliant one.
FIRST MARQUIS:
    Oh, yes, all our own people—the gay world!
    (*They name the ladies who enter the boxes elaborately dressed.
    Bows and smiles are exchanged*)
SECOND MARQUIS: Madame de Guéméné . . .
CUIGY:                De Bois-Dauphin . . .
FIRST MARQUIS: Whom we adore—
BRISSAILLE:           Madame de Chavigny . . .
SECOND MARQUIS: Who plays with all our hearts—
LIGNIÈRE:            Why, there's Corneille
    Returned from Rouen!
THE BOY (*to his father*):        Are the Academy
    All here?
THE CITIZEN: I see some of them . . . there's Boudu—
    Boissat—Cureau—Porchères—Colomby—

Bourzeys—Bourdon—Arbaut—

        Ah, those great names,
Never to be forgotten!

FIRST MARQUIS:      Look—at last!
Our Intellectuals! Barthénoide,
Urimédonte, Félixérie . . .

SECOND MARQUIS (*languishing*):   Sweet heaven!
How exquisite their surnames are! Marquis,
You know them all?

FIRST MARQUIS:   I know them all, Marquis!

LIGNIÈRE (*draws* CHRISTIAN *aside*):
My dear boy, I came here to serve you— Well,
But where's the lady? I'll be going.

CHRISTIAN:       Not yet—
A little longer! She is always here.
Please! I must find some way of meeting her.
I am dying of love! And you—you know
Everyone, the whole court and the whole town,
And put them all into your songs—at least
You can tell me her name!

THE FIRST VIOLIN (*raps on his desk with his bow*): Pst—
Gentlemen!      (*raises his bow*)

THE ORANGE GIRL: Macaroons, lemonade—

CHRISTIAN:      Then she may be
One of those æsthetes . . . Intellectuals,
You call them— How can I talk to a woman
In that style? I have no wit. This fine manner
Of speaking and of writing nowadays—
Not for me! I am a soldier—and afraid.
That's her box, on the right—the empty one.

LIGNIÈRE (*starts for the door*): I am going.

CHRISTIAN (*restrains him*): No—wait!

LIGNIÈRE:     Not I. There's a tavern
Not far away—and I am dying of thirst.

THE ORANGE GIRL (*passes with her tray*): Orange juice?

LIGNIÈRE:                                                 No!
THE ORANGE GIRL: Milk?
LIGNIÈRE:                   Pouah!
THE ORANGE GIRL:                   Muscatel?
LIGNIÈRE:                                         Here! Stop!
    (*to* CHRISTIAN): I'll stay a little.
    (*to the girl*):                         Let me see
    Your Muscatel.
    (*He sits down by the sideboard. The girl pours out wine for him*)
VOICES (*in the crowd about the door, upon the entrance of a*
    *spruce little man, rather fat, with a beaming smile*):
    Ragueneau!
LIGNIÈRE (*to* CHRISTIAN):                         Ragueneau,
    Poet and pastry-cook—a character!
RAGUENEAU (*dressed like a confectioner in his Sunday clothes,*
    *advances quickly to* LIGNIÈRE):
    Sir, have you seen Monsieur de Cyrano?
LIGNIÈRE (*presents him to* CHRISTIAN):
    Permit me . . . Ragueneau, confectioner,
    The chief support of modern poetry.
RAGUENEAU (*bridling*): Oh—too much honour!
LIGNIÈRE:                         Patron of the Arts—
    Mæcenas! Yes, you are—
RAGUENEAU:                                   Undoubtedly,
    The poets gather round my hearth.
LIGNIÈRE                                         On credit—
    Himself a poet—
RAGUENEAU:             So they say—
LIGNIÈRE:                                         Maintains
    The Muses.
RAGUENEAU:                   It is true that for an ode—
LIGNIÈRE: You give a tart—
RAGUENEAU:             A tartlet—
LIGNIÈRE:                                         Modesty!
    And for a triolet you give—

RAGUENEAU:                    Plain bread.

LIGNIÈRE (*severely*):
  Bread and milk! And you love the theatre?

RAGUENEAU: I adore it!

LIGNIÈRE:                    Well, pastry pays for all.
  Your place to-day now—Come, between ourselves,
  What did it cost you?

RAGUENEAU:                    Four pies; fourteen cakes.
  (*Looking about*)
  But— Cyrano not here? Astonishing!

LIGNIÈRE: Why so?

RAGUENEAU:          Why— Montfleury plays!

LIGNIÈRE:                              Yes, I hear
  That hippopotamus assumes the rôle
  Of Phédon. What is that to Cyrano?

RAGUENEAU:
  Have you not heard? Monsieur de Bergerac
  So hates Montfleury, he has forbidden him
  For three weeks to appear upon the stage.

LIGNIÈRE (*who is, by this time, at his fourth glass*): Well?

RAGUENEAU: Montfleury plays!—

CUIGY (*strolls over to them*):      Yes—what then?

RAGUENEAU:                              Ah! That
  Is what I came to see.

FIRST MARQUIS:                          This Cyrano—
  Who is he?

CUIGY:          Oh, he is the lad with the long sword.

SECOND MARQUIS: Noble?

CUIGY:                Sufficiently; he is in the Guards.
  (*Points to a gentleman who comes and goes about the hall as
  though seeking for someone*)
  His friend Le Bret can tell you more. Le Bret!
  (LE BRET *comes down to them*)
  Looking for Bergerac?

LE BRET:                Yes. And for trouble.

CUIGY: Is he not an extraordinary man?

LE BRET: The best friend and the bravest soul alive!

RAGUENEAU: Poet—

CUIGY:                    Swordsman—

LE BRET:                              Musician—

BRISSAILLE:                                        Philosopher—

LIGNIÈRE: Such a remarkable appearance, too!

RAGUENEAU:

Truly, I should not look to find his portrait
By the grave hand of Philippe de Champagne.
He might have been a model for Callot—
One of those wild swashbucklers in a masque—
Hat with three plumes, and doublet with six points—
His cloak behind him over his long sword
Cocked, like the tail of strutting Chanticleer—
Prouder than all the swaggering Tamburlaines
Hatched out of Gascony. And to complete
This Punchinello figure—such a nose!—
My lords, there is no such nose as that nose—
You cannot look upon it without crying: "Oh, no,
Impossible! Exaggerated!" Then
You smile, and say: "Of course— I might have known;
Presently he will take it off." But that
Monsieur de Bergerac will never do.

LIGNIÈRE (*grimly*):

He keeps it—and God help the man who smiles!

RAGUENEAU: His sword is one half of the shears of Fate!

FIRST MARQUIS (*shrugs*): He will not come.

RAGUENEAU:                              Will he not? Sir, I'll lay you
A pullet à la Ragueneau!

FIRST MARQUIS (*laughing*): Done!

(*Murmurs of admiration;* ROXANE *has just appeared in her box. She sits at the front of the box, and her Duenna takes a seat toward the rear.* CHRISTIAN, *busy paying the Orange Girl, does not see her at first*)

SECOND MARQUIS (*with little excited cries*):                    Ah!
    Oh! Oh! Sweet sirs, look yonder! Is she not
    Frightfully ravishing?
FIRST MARQUIS:                    Bloom of the peach—
    Blush of the strawberry—
SECOND MARQUIS:                    So fresh—so cool,
    That our hearts, grown all warm with loving her,
    May catch their death of cold!
CHRISTIAN (*looks up, sees* ROXANE, *and seizes* LIGNIÈRE *by
    the arm*):                    There! Quick—up there—
    In the box! Look!—
LIGNIÈRE (*coolly*):        Herself?
CHRISTIAN:                    Quickly— Her name?
LIGNIÈRE (*sipping his wine, and speaking between sips*):
    Madeleine  Robin,  called  Roxane . . . refined . . .
    Intellectual . . .
CHRISTIAN:        Ah!—
LIGNIÈRE:        Unmarried . . .
CHRISTIAN:                    Oh!—
LIGNIÈRE: No title . . . rich enough . . . an orphan . . .
    cousin
    To Cyrano . . . of whom we spoke just now . . .
    (*At this point, a very distinguished-looking gentleman, the
    Cordon Bleu around his neck, enters the box, and stands a
    moment talking with* ROXANE)
CHRISTIAN (*starts*): And the man? . . .
LIGNIÈRE (*beginning to feel his wine a little; cocks his eye at them*):
    Oho! That man? . . . Comte de Guiche . . .
    In love with her . . . married himself, however,
    To the niece of the Cardinal—Richelieu . . .
    Wishes Roxane, therefore, to marry one
    Monsieur  de  Valvert . . . Vicomte . . . friend  of
    his . . .
    A somewhat melancholy gentleman . . .
    But . . . well, accommodating! . . . She says No . . .

Nevertheless, de Guiche is powerful . . .
Not above persecuting . . .
(*he rises, swaying a little, and very happy*)

I have written
A little song about his little game . . .
Good little song, too . . . Here, I'll sing it for you . . .
Make de Guiche furious . . . naughty little song . . .
Not so bad, either— Listen! . . .
(*he stands with his glass held aloft, ready to sing*)

CHRISTIAN:                                          No. Adieu.

LIGNIÈRE: Whither away?

CHRISTIAN:                  To Monsieur de Valvert!

LIGNIÈRE: Careful! The man's a swordsman . . .
(*nods toward* ROXANE, *who is watching* CHRISTIAN)

Wait! Someone
Looking at you—

CHRISTIAN:                  Roxane! . . .
(*He forgets everything, and stands spellbound, gazing toward* ROXANE. *The Cut-Purse and his crew, observing him transfixed, his eyes raised and his mouth half open, begin edging in his direction*)

LIGNIÈRE:                                    Oh! Very well,
Then I'll be leaving you . . . Good day . . . Good
      day! . . .
(CHRISTIAN *remains motionless*)
Everywhere else, they like to hear me sing!—
Also, I am thirsty.
(*He goes out, navigating carefully.* LE BRET, *having made the circuit of the hall, returns to* RAGUENEAU, *somewhat reassured*)

LE BRET:                                    No sign anywhere
Of Cyrano!

RAGUENEAU (*incredulous*): Wait and see!

LE BRET:                                    Humph! I hope
He has not seen the bill.

THE CROWD:                                    The play!—The play!—

FIRST MARQUIS (*observing* DE GUICHE, *as he descends from*
  ROXANE'S *box and crosses the floor, followed by a knot of*
  *obsequious gentlemen, the* VICOMTE DE VALVERT *among*
  *them*):

  This man de Guiche—what ostentation!

SECOND MARQUIS:                                    Bah!—
  Another Gascon!

FIRST MARQUIS:                          Gascon, yes—but cold
  And calculating—certain to succeed—
  My word for it. Come, shall we make our bow?
  We shall be none the worse, I promise you . . .
  (*they go toward* DE GUICHE)

SECOND MARQUIS:
  Beautiful ribbons, Count! That colour, now,
  What is it—"Kiss-me-Dear" or "Startled-Fawn"?

DE GUICHE: I call that shade "The Dying Spaniard."

FIRST MARQUIS:                                    Ha!
  And no false colours either—thanks to you
  And your brave troops, in Flanders before long
  The Spaniard will die daily.

DE GUICHE:                            Shall we go
  And sit upon the stage? Come Valvert.

CHRISTIAN (*starts at the name*):            Valvert!—
  The Vicomte— Ah, that scoundrel! Quick—my
      glove—
  I'll throw it in his face—
  (*reaching into his pocket for his glove, he catches the hand of*
  *the Cut-Purse*)

THE CUT-PURSE: Oh!—

CHRISTIAN (*holding fast to the man's wrist*):    Who are you?
  I was looking for a glove—

THE CUT-PURSE (*cringing*):            You found a hand.
  (*Hurriedly*)
  Let me go—I can tell you something—

CHRISTIAN (*still holding him*):                                    Well?

THE CUT-PURSE: Lignière—that friend of yours—

CHRISTIAN:                                                          Well?

THE CUT-PURSE:                                          Good as dead—
    Understand? Ambuscaded. Wrote a song
    About—no matter. There's a hundred men
    Waiting for him to-night—I'm one of them.

CHRISTIAN: A hundred! Who arranged this?

THE CUT-PURSE:                                             Secret.

CHRISTIAN:                                                           Oh!

THE CUT-PURSE: Professional secret.

CHRISTIAN:                                        Where are they to be?

THE CUT-PURSE:
    Porte de Nesle. On his way home. Tell him so.
    Save his life.

CHRISTIAN (*releases the man*):
    Yes, but where am I to find him?

THE CUT-PURSE:
    Go round the taverns. There's the Golden Grape,
    The Pineapple, the Bursting Belt, the Two
    Torches, the Three Funnels—in every one
    You leave a line of writing—understand?
    To warn him.

CHRISTIAN (*starts for the door*):
                    I'll go! God, what swine—a hundred
    Against one man! . . .
    (*Stops and looks longingly at* ROXANE)
                        Leave *her* here!—
    (*Savagely, turning toward* VALVERT)

                        And leave *him*!—
    (*Decidedly*)
    I must save Lignière!
    (*Exit*)
    (DE GUICHE, VALVERT, *and all the Marquis have disappeared
    through the curtains, to take their seats upon the stage. The*

*floor is entirely filled; not a vacant seat remains in the gallery or in the boxes)*

THE CROWD:                              The play! The play! Begin the play!

A CITIZEN (*as his wig is hoisted into the air on the end of a fishline, in the hands of a page in the gallery*):   My wig!!

CRIES OF JOY:                              He's bald! Bravo, You Pages! Ha ha ha!

THE CITIZEN:            Here, you young villain!

CRIES AND LAUGHTER: HA HA! Ha Ha! ha ha. . . .
    (*Complete silence*

LE BRET (*surprised*):              That sudden hush? . . .
    (*A spectator whispers in his ear*)
    Yes?

THE SPECTATOR: I was told on good authority . . .

MURMURS (*here and there*)
    What? . . . Here? . . . No . . . Yes . . . Look—in the latticed box—
    The Cardinal! . . . The Cardinal! . . .

A PAGE:                              The Devil!—
    Now we shall all have to behave ourselves!
    (*Three raps on the stage. The audience becomes motionless. Silence*)

THE VOICE OF A MARQUIS (*from the stage, behind the curtains*):
    Snuff that candle!

ANOTHER MARQUIS (*puts his head out through the curtains*):
                              A chair! . . .
    (*A chair is passed from hand to hand over the heads of the crowd. He takes it, and disappears behind the curtains, not without having blown a few kisses to the occupants of the boxes*)

A SPECTATOR:            Silence!

VOICES:                              Hssh! . . . Hssh! . . .
    (*Again the three raps on the stage. The curtains part. Tableau. The Marquis seated on their chairs to right and left*

*of the stage, insolently posed. Back drop representing a
pastoral scene, bluish in tone. Four little crystal chandeliers
light up the stage. The violins play softly)*

LE BRET (*in a low tone, to* RAGUENEAU):
Montfleury enters now?

RAGUENEAU (*nods*):          Opens the play.

LE BRET (*much relieved*): Then Cyrano is not here!

RAGUENEAU:                                    I lose . . .

LE BRET:                                        Humph!—
So much the better!
(*The melody of a Gavotte is heard.* MONTFLEURY *appears
upon the scene, a ponderous figure in the costume of a rustic
shepherd, a hat garlanded with roses tilted over one ear,
playing upon a beribboned pastoral pipe*)

THE CROWD:          Montfleury! . . . Bravo! . . .

MONTFLEURY (*after bowing to the applause, begins the rôle of
Phédon*):
"Thrice happy he who hides from pomp and power
In sylvan shade or solitary bower;
Where balmy zephyrs fan his burning cheeks—"

A VOICE (*from the midst of the hall*):
Wretch! Have I not forbade you these three weeks?
(*Sensation. Every one turns to look. Murmurs*)

SEVERAL VOICES: What? . . . Where? . . . Who is it? . . .

CUIGY: Cyrano!

LE BRET (*in alarm*): Himself!

THE VOICE: King of clowns! Leave the stage—*at once*!

THE CROWD:                                    Oh!—

MONTFLEURY:                                    Now,
Now, now—

THE VOICE:      You disobey me?

SEVERAL VOICES (*from the floor, from the boxes*): Hsh! Go on—
Quiet!—Go on, Montfleury!—Who's afraid?—

MONTFLEURY (*in a voice of no great assurance*):
"Thrice happy he who hides from . . ."

THE VOICE (*more menacingly*):        Well? Well? Well? . . .
  Monarch of mountebanks! Must I come and plant
  A forest on your shoulders?
  (*A cane at the end of a long arm shakes above the heads of the crowd*)
MONTFLEURY (*in a voice increasingly feeble*):
                          "Thrice hap——"
  (*The cane is violently agitated*)
THE VOICE:                                      *GO!!!*
THE CROWD: Ah! . . .
CYRANO (*arises in the centre of the floor, erect upon a chair, his arms folded, his hat cocked ferociously, his moustache bristling, his nose terrible*):
                    Presently I shall grow angry!
MONTFLEURY (*to the Marquis*):              Messieurs,
  If you protect me—
A MARQUIS (*nonchalantly*): Well—proceed!
CYRANO:                                  Fat swine!
  If you dare breathe one balmy zephyr more,
  *I'll* fan your cheeks for you!
THE MARQUIS:              Quiet down there!
CYRANO:
  Unless these gentlemen retain their seats,
  My cane may bite their ribbons!
ALL THE MARQUIS:                    That will do!—
  Montfleury—
CYRANO:          Fly, goose! Shoo! Take to your wings,
  Before I pluck your plumes, and draw your gorge!
A VOICE: See here!—
CYRANO:        Off stage!!
ANOTHER VOICE:          One moment—
CYRANO:                  What—still there?
  (*turns back his cuffs deliberately*)
  Very good—then I enter—*Left—with knife*—
  To carve this large Italian sausage.

MONTFLEURY (*desperately attempting dignity*):                Sir,
  When you insult me, you insult the Muse!
CYRANO (*with great politeness*):
  Sir, if the Muse, who never knew your name,
  Had the honour to meet you—then be sure
  That after one glance at that face of yours,
  That figure of a mortuary urn—
  She would apply her buskin—toward the rear!
THE CROWD:
  Montfleury! . . . Montfleury! . . . The play! The
      play!
CYRANO (*to those who are shouting and crowding about him*):
  Pray you, be gentle with my scabbard here—
  She'll put her tongue out at you presently!—
THE CROWD (*recoiling*): Keep back—
CYRANO (*to* MONTFLEURY):            Begone!
THE CROWD (*pushing in closer, and growling*):
                                Ahr! . . . ahr! . . .
CYRANO (*turns upon them*):            Did someone speak?
    (*They recoil again*)
A VOICE (*in the back of the hall, sings*):
            Monsieur de Cyrano
              Must be another Caesar—
            Let Brutus lay him low,
              And play us "La Clorise"!
ALL THE CROWD (*singing*): "La Clorise!" "La Clorise!"
CYRANO:
  Let me hear one more word of that same song,
  And I destroy you all!
A CITIZEN:                          Who might you be?
  Samson?—
CYRANO:              Precisely. Would you kindly lend me
  Your jawbone?
A LADY:            What an outrage!
A NOBLE:                        Scandalous!

A Citizen: Annoying!

A Page: What a game!

The Crowd: Kss! Montfleury!
Cyrano!

Cyrano: Silence!

The Crowd: Woof! Woof! Baaa! Cockadoo!

Cyrano: I—

A Page: Meow!

Cyrano: I say be silent!—
(*His voice dominates the uproar*)
And I offer
One universal challenge to you all!
Approach, young heroes—I will take your names.
Each in his turn—no crowding! One, two, three—
Come, get your numbers—who will head the list—
You sir? No— You? Ah, no. To the first man
Who falls I'll build a monument! . . . Not one?
Will all who wish to die, please raise their hands? . . .
I see. You are so modest, you might blush
Before a sword naked. Sweet innocence! . . .
Not one name? Not one finger? . . . Very well,
Then I go on:
(*turning back toward the stage, where* Montfleury *waits in despair*)
I'd have our theatre cured
Of this carbuncle. Or if not, why then—
(*his hand on his sword hilt*)
The lancet!

Montfleury: I—

Cyrano (*descends from his chair, seats himself comfortably in the centre of the circle which has formed around him, and makes himself quite at home*):
Attend to me—full moon!
I clap my hands, three times—thus. At the third
You will eclipse yourself.

THE CROWD (*amused*):        Ah!

CYRANO:                Ready? One!

MONTFLEURY: I—

A VOICE (*from the boxes*): No!

THE CROWD:                He'll go— He'll stay—

MONTFLEURY:                I really think,
    Gentlemen—

CYRANO:        Two!

MONTFLEURY:        Perhaps I had better—

CYRANO:                        Three!

(MONTFLEURY *disappears, as if through a trapdoor. Tempest of laughter, hoots and hisses*)

THE CROWD: Yah!—Coward— Come back—

CYRANO (*beaming, drops back in his chair and crosses his legs*):
                        Let him—if he dare!

A CITIZEN: The Manager! Speech! Speech!

    (BELLEROSE *advances and bows*)

THE BOXES:                Ah! Bellerose!

BELLEROSE (*with elegance*): Most noble—most fair—

THE CROWD:                No! The Comedian—
    Jodelet!—

JODELET (*advances, and speaks through his nose*)
            Lewd fellows of the baser sort—

THE CROWD: Ha! Ha! Not bad! Bravo!

JODELET:                No Bravos here!
    Our heavy tragedian with the voluptuous bust
    Was taken suddenly—

THE CROWD:        Yah! Coward!

JODELET:                I mean . . .
    He had to be excused—

THE CROWD:                Call him back— No!—
    Yes!—

THE BOY (*to* CYRANO):
            After all, Monsieur, what reason have you
    To hate this Montfleury?

CYRANO (*graciously, still seated*):          My dear young man,
    I have two reasons, either one alone
    Conclusive. *Primo:* A lamentable actor,
    Who mouths his verse and moans his tragedy,
    And heaves up— Ugh!—like a hod-carrier, lines
    That ought to soar on their own wings. *Secundo:*—
    Well—that's my secret.
THE OLD CITIZEN (*behind him*):     But you close the play—
    "La Clorise"—by Baro! Are we to miss
    Our entertainment, merely—
CYRANO (*respectfully, turns his chair toward the old man*):

                            My dear old boy,
    The poetry of Baro being worth
    Zero, or less, I feel that I have done
    Poetic justice!
THE INTELLECTUALS (*in the boxes*):     Really!—our Baro!—
    My dear!—Who ever?—Ah, dieu! The idea!—
CYRANO (*gallantly, turns his chair toward the boxes*):
    Fair ladies—shine upon us like the sun,
    Blossom like flowers around us—be our songs,
    Heard in a dream— Make sweet the hour of death,
    Smiling upon us as you close our eyes—
    Inspire, but do not try to criticise!
BELLEROSE:
    Quite so!—and the mere money—possibly
    You would like that returned— Yes?
CYRANO:                                        Bellerose,
    You speak the first word of intelligence!
    I will not wound the mantle of the Muse—
    Here, catch!—
    (*throws him a purse*)
              And hold your tongue.
THE CROWD (*astonished*):               Ah! Ah!
JODELET (*deftly catches the purse, weighs it in his hand*):
                            Monsieur,

You are hereby authorized to close our play
Every night, on the same terms.

THE CROWD:                              Boo!

JODELET:                                 And welcome!
Let us be booed together, you and I!

BELLEROSE: Kindly pass out quietly . . .

JODELET (*burlesquing* BELLEROSE):      Quietly . . .
(*They begin to go out, while* CYRANO *looks about him with
satisfaction. But the exodus ceases presently during the
ensuing scene. The ladies in the boxes who have already risen
and put on their wraps, stop to listen, and finally sit down
again*)

LE BRET (*to* CYRANO): Idiot!

A MEDDLER (*hurries up to* CYRANO):
                        But what a scandal! Montfleury—
The great Montfleury! Did you know the Duc
De Candale was his patron? Who is yours?

CYRANO: No one.

THE MEDDLER:  No one—no patron?

CYRANO:                          I said no.

THE MEDDLER:
What, no great lord, to cover with his name—

CYRANO (*with visible annoyance*):
No, I have told you twice. Must I repeat?
No, sir, no patron—          (*his hand on his sword*)
                    But a patroness!

THE MEDDLER: And when do you leave Paris?

CYRANO:                          That's as may be.

THE MEDDLER: The Duc de Candale has a long arm.

CYRANO:                                   Mine
Is longer
(*drawing his sword*)
              by three feet of steel.

THE MEDDLER:                              Yes, yes,
But do you dream of daring—

CYRANO:                                              I do dream
    Of daring . . .
THE MEDDLER:      But—
CYRANO:                      You may go now.
THE MEDDLER:                                      But—
CYRANO:                                          You may go—
    Or tell me why are you staring at my nose!
THE MEDDLER (*in confusion*): No—I—
CYRANO (*stepping up to him*):        Does it astonish you?
THE MEDDLER (*drawing back*):                    Your grace
    Misunderstands my—
CYRANO:                          Is it long and soft
    And dangling, like a trunk?
THE MEDDLER:                    I never said—
CYRANO: Or crooked, like an owl's beak?
THE MEDDLER:                          I—
CYRANO:                                          Perhaps
    A pimple ornaments the end of it?
THE MEDDLER: No—
CYRANO:                      Or a fly parading up and down?
    What is this portent?
THE MEDDLER:          Oh!—
CYRANO:                          This phenomenon?
THE MEDDLER: But I have been careful not to look—
CYRANO:                                          And why
    Not, if you please?
THE MEDDLER:          Why—
CYRANO:                      It disgusts you, then?
THE MEDDLER: My dear sir—
CYRANO:                      Does its colour appear to you
    Unwholesome?
THE MEDDLER:      Oh, by no means!
CYRANO:                                      Or its form
    Obscene?
THE MEDDLER: Not in the least—

CYRANO:                                    Then why assume
    This deprecating manner? Possibly
    You find it just a trifle large?
THE MEDDLER:                               Oh, no!—
    Small, very small, infinitesimal—
CYRANO (*roars*)                              What!
    How? You accuse me of absurdity?
    Small—*my nose*? Why—
THE MEDDLER:            My God!—
CYRANO:                                Magnificent,
    My nose! . . . You pug, you knob, you button-head,
    Know that I glory in this nose of mine,
    For a great nose indicates a great man—
    Genial, courteous, intellectual,
    Virile, courageous—as I am—and such
    As you—poor wretch—will never dare to be
    Even in imagination. For that face—
    That blank, inglorious concavity
    Which my right hand finds—          (*he strikes him*)
THE MEDDLER:            Ow!
CYRANO:                            —on top of you,
    Is as devoid of pride, of poetry,
    Of soul, of picturesqueness, of contour,
    Of character, of NOSE in short—as that
    (*takes him by the shoulders and turns him around, suiting
    the action to the word*)
    Which at the end of that limp spine of yours
    My left foot—
THE MEDDLER (*escaping*): Help! The Guard!
CYRANO:                            Take notice all
    Who find this feature of my countenance
    A theme for comedy! When the humorist
    Is noble, then my custom is to show
    Appreciation proper to his rank—
    More heartfelt . . . and more pointed. . . .

DE GUICHE (*who has come down from the stage, surrounded by the Marquis*):                              Presently
   This fellow will grow tiresome.

VALVERT:                                          Oh, he blows
   His trumpet!

DE GUICHE:       Well—will no one interfere?

VALVERT: No one?
   (*Looks round*)
                              Observe. I myself will proceed
   To put him in his place.
   (*He walks up to* CYRANO, *who has been watching him, and stands there, looking him over with an affected air*)
                        Ah . . . your nose . . . hem! . . .
   Your nose is . . . rather large!

CYRANO (*gravely*):                        Rather.

VALVERT (*simpering*):                        Oh, well—

CYRANO (*coolly*): Is that all?

VALVERT (*turns away, with a shrug*): Well, of course—

CYRANO:      .                          Ah, no, young sir!
   You are too simple. Why, you might have said—
   Oh, a great many things! Mon dieu, why waste
   Your opportunity? For example, thus:—
   AGGRESSIVE: I, sir, if that nose were mine,
   I'd have it amputated—on the spot!
   FRIENDLY: How do you drink with such a nose?
   You ought to have a cup made specially.
   DESCRIPTIVE: 'Tis a rock—a crag—a cape—
   A cape? say rather, a peninsula!
   INQUISITIVE: What is that receptacle—
   A razor-case or a portfolio?
   KINDLY: Ah, do you love the little birds
   So much that when they come and sing to you,
   You give them this to perch on? INSOLENT:
   Sir, when you smoke, the neighbours must suppose
   Your chimney is on fire. CAUTIOUS: Take care—

2

A weight like that might make you topheavy.
THOUGHTFUL: Somebody fetch my parasol—
Those delicate colours fade so in the sun!
PEDANTIC: Does not Aristophanes
Mention a mythologic monster called
Hippocampelephantocamelos?
Surely we have here the original!
FAMILIAR: Well, old torchlight! Hang your hat
Over that chandelier—it hurts my eyes.
ELOQUENT: When it blows, the typhoon howls,
And the clouds darken. DRAMATIC: When it bleeds—
The Red Sea! ENTERPRISING: What a sign
For some perfumer! LYRIC: Hark—the horn
Of Roland calls to summon Charlemagne!—
SIMPLE: When do they unveil the monument?
RESPECTFUL: Sir, I recognize in you
A man of parts, a man of prominence—
RUSTIC: Hey? What? Call that a nose? Na, na—
I be no fool like what you think I be—
That there's a blue cucumber! MILITARY:
Point against cavalry! PRACTICAL: Why not
A lottery with this for the grand prize?
Or—parodying Faustus in the play—
"Was this the nose that launched a thousand ships
And burned the topless towers of Ilium?"
These, my dear sir, are things you might have said
Had you some tinge of letters, or of wit
To colour your discourse. But wit,—not so,
You never had an atom—and of letters,
You need but three to write you down—an Ass.
Moreover,—if you had the invention, here
Before these folk to make a jest of me—
Be sure you would not then articulate
The twentieth part of half a syllable
Of the beginning! For I say these things

Lightly enough myself, about myself,
But I allow none else to utter them.

DE GUICHE (*tries to lead away the amazed* VALVERT):
Vicomte—come.

VALVERT:                    Oh— These arrogant grand airs!—
A clown who—look at him—not even gloves!
No ribbons—no lace—no buckles on his shoes—

CYRANO:
I carry my adornments on my soul.
I do not dress up like a popinjay;
But inwardly, I keep my daintiness.
I do not bear with me, by any chance,
An insult not yet washed away—a conscience
Yellow with unpurged bile—an honour frayed
To rags, a set of scruples badly worn.
I go caparisoned in gems unseen,
Trailing white plumes of freedom, garlanded
With my good name—no figure of a man,
But a soul clothed in shining armour, hung
With deeds for decorations, twirling—thus—
A bristling wit, and swinging at my side
Courage, and on the stones of this old town
Making the sharp truth ring, like golden spurs!

VALVERT: But—

CYRANO:                    But I have no gloves! A pity too!
I had one—the last one of an old pair—
And lost that. Very careless of me. Some
Gentleman offered me an impertinence.
I left it—in his face.

VALVERT:                    Dolt, bumpkin, fool,
Insolent puppy, jobbernowl!

CYRANO (*removes his hat and bows*):                    Ah, yes?
And I—Cyrano-Savinien-Hercule
De Bergerac!

VALVERT (*turns away*): Buffoon!

CYRANO (*cries out as if suddenly taken with a cramp*):     Oh!

VALVERT (*turns back*): Well, what now?

CYRANO (*with grimaces of anguish*):

> I must do something to relieve these cramps—
> This is what comes of lack of exercise—
> Ah!—

VALVERT: What is all this?

CYRANO:                     My sword has gone to sleep!

VALVERT (*draws*): So be it!

CYRANO:                     You shall die exquisitely.

VALVERT (*contemptuously*): Poet!

CYRANO:                     Why yes, a poet, if you will;

> So while we fence, I'll make you a Ballade
> Extempore.

VALVERT:          A Ballade?

CYRANO:                          Yes. You know

> What that is?

VALVERT:      I—

CYRANO:                     The Ballade, sir, is formed

> Of three stanzas of eight lines each—

VALVERT:                     Oh, come!

CYRANO: And a refrain of four.

VALVERT:                You—

CYRANO:                                    I'll compose

> One, while I fight with you; and at the end
> Of the last line—thrust home!

VALVERT:                     Will you?

CYRANO:                                    I will.

> (*declaims*)
> "Ballade of the duel at the Hôtel de Bourgogne
>     Between de Bergerac and a Boeotian."

VALVERT (*sneering*): What do you mean by that?

CYRANO:                     Oh, that? The title.

THE CROWD (*excited*): Come on—

>                     A circle—

THE CROWD (*excited*):                    Quiet—
                                                    Down in front!
(*Tableau. A ring of interested spectators in the centre of the
floor, the Marquis and the Officers mingling with the citizens
and common folk. Pages swarming up on men's shoulders to
see better; the Ladies in the boxes standing and leaning over.
To the right,* DE GUICHE *and his following; to the left,* LE
BRET, CUIGY, RAGUENEAU, *and others of* CYRANO'S *friends*)
CYRANO (*closes his eyes for an instant*):
        Stop . . . Let me choose my rhyme. . . . Now!
            Here we go—
        (*He suits the action to the word, throughout the following*):

Lightly I toss my hat away,
    Languidly over my arm let fall
The cloak that covers my bright array—
    Then out swords, and to work withal!
    A Launcelot, in his Lady's hall . . .
    A Spartacus, at the Hippodrome! . . .
    I dally awhile with you, dear jackal,
Then, as I end the refrain, thrust home!

(*The swords cross—the fight is on*)

Where shall I skewer my peacock . . . Nay,
    Better for you to have shunned this brawl!—
Here, in the heart, thro' your ribbons gay?
    —In the belly, under your silken shawl?
    Hark, how the steel rings musical!
Mark how my point floats, light as the foam,
    Ready to drive you back to the wall,
Then, as I end the refrain, thrust home!

Ho, for a rhyme! . . . You are white as whey—
    You break, you cower, you cringe, you . . . crawl!
Tac!—and I parry your last essay:
    So may the turn of a hand forestall
    Life with its honey, death with its gall;

So may the turn of my fancy roam
   Free, for a time, till the rhymes recall,
Then, as I end the refrain, thrust home!

   (*He announces solemnly*)

Refrain:
   Prince! Pray God, that is Lord of all,
Pardon your soul, for your time has come!
   Beat—pass—fling you aslant, asprawl—
Then, as I end the refrain . . .
   (*He lunges;* VALVERT *staggers back and falls into the arms
   of his friends.* CYRANO *recovers, and salutes*)
                                             —Thrust home!
   (*Shouts. Applause from the boxes. Flowers and hand-
   kerchiefs come fluttering down. The Officers surround*
   CYRANO *and congratulate him.* RAGUENEAU *dances for joy.*
   LE BRET *is unable to conceal his enthusiasm. The friends of*
   VALVERT *hold him up and help him away*)

THE CROWD (*in one long cry*): Ah-h!
A CAVALIER:                              Superb!
A WOMAN:                                          Simply sweet!
RAGUENEAU: Magnelephant!
A MARQUIS:                        A novelty!
LE BRET:                                          Bah!
THE CROWD (*thronging around* CYRANO):
                                   Compliments—regards—
   Bravo!—
A WOMAN'S VOICE: Why, he's a hero!
A MUSKETEER (*advances quickly to* CYRANO, *with outstretched
   hands*):                              Monsieur, will you
   Permit me?—It was altogether fine!
   I think I may appreciate these things—
   Moreover, I have been stamping for pure joy!
   (*He retires quickly*)
CYRANO (*to* CUIGY): What was that gentleman's name?

CUIGY: Oh . . . D'Artagnan.
LE BRET (*takes* CYRANO's *arm*): Come here and tell me—
CYRANO:                          Let this crowd go first—
    (*to* BELLEROSE)
    May we stay?
BELLEROSE (*with great respect*): Certainly!
    (*Cries and cat-calls off stage*)
JODELET (*comes down from the door where he has been looking out*):
                        Hark!— Montfleury—
    They are hooting him.
BELLEROSE (*solemnly*):      "Sic transit gloria!"
    (*Changes his tone and shouts to the Porter and the Lamplighter*)
    —Strike! . . . Close the house! . . . Leave the
        lights— We rehearse
    The new farce after dinner.
    (JODELET *and* BELLEROSE *go out after elaborately saluting*
    CYRANO.)
THE PORTER (*to* CYRANO):      You do not dine?
CYRANO: I?—No!
    (*The Porter turns away*)
LE BRET:      Why not?
CYRANO (*haughtily*):      Because—
    (*changing his tone when he sees the Porter has gone*)
                      Because I have
    No money.
LE BRET (*gesture of teasing*): But—the purse of gold?
CYRANO:                          Farewell,
    Paternal pension!
LE BRET:            So you have, until
    The first of next month—?
CYRANO:                    Nothing.
LE BRET:                          What a fool!—
CYRANO: But—what a gesture!
THE ORANGE GIRL (*behind her little counter; coughs*):
                    Hem!

(CYRANO *and* LE BRET *look around; she advances timidly*):

                          Pardon, monsieur . . .

A man ought never to go hungry . . .

(*indicating the sideboard*)

                                  See,

I have everything here . . .

(*eagerly*)                   Please!—

CYRANO:                     My dear child,

I cannot bend this Gascon pride of mine

To accept such a kindness— Yet, for fear

That I may give you pain if I refuse,

I will take . . .

(*he goes to the sideboard and makes his selection*)

                 Oh, not very much! A grape . . .

(*she gives him the bunch; he removes a single grape*)

One only! And a glass of water . . .

(*she starts to pour wine into it; he stops her*)

Clear!   And . . . half a macaroon!

(*he gravely returns the other half*)

LE BRET:                Old idiot!

THE ORANGE GIRL: Please!—Nothing more?

CYRANO               Why yes— Your hand to kiss.

(*He kisses the hand which she holds out, as he would the hand of a princess*)

THE ORANGE GIRL: Thank you, sir.

(*She curtseys*)            Good-night.

(*She goes out*)

CYRANO: Now, I am listening.

(*plants himself before the sideboard and arranges thereon—*)

Dinner!—

(*—the macaroon*)

         Drink!—

(*—the glass of water*)

                Dessert!—

(*—the grape*)

CYRANO                         There—now I'll sit down.
> *(Seats himself)*
> Lord, I was hungry! Abominably!
> *(Eating)*                         Well?

LE BRET:
> These fatheads with the bellicose grand airs
> Will have you ruined if you listen to them;
> Talk to a man of sense and hear how all
> Your swagger impresses him.

CYRANO *(finishes his macaroon)*:       Enormously.

LE BRET: The Cardinal—

CYRANO *(beaming)*:       Was he there?

LE BRET:                         He must have thought you—

CYRANO: Original.

LE BRET:       Well, but—

CYRANO:                         He is himself
> A playwright. He will not be too displeased
> That I have closed another author's play.

LE BRET: But look at all the enemies you have made!

CYRANO *(begins on the grape)*: How   many — do   you
>   think?

LE BRET:                         Just forty-eight
> Without the women.

CYRANO:                  Count them.

LE BRET:                         Montfleury,
> Baro, de Guiche, the Vicomte, the Old Man,
> All the Academy—

CYRANO:                  Enough! You make me
>   Happy!

LE BRET:    But where is all this leading you?
> What is your plan?

CYRANO:                  I have been wandering—
> Wasting my force upon too many plans.
> Now I have chosen one.

LE BRET:                  What one?

> 2*

CYRANO:                                The simplest—
    To make myself in all things admirable!
LE BRET:
    Hmph!—Well, then, the real reason why you hate
    Montfleury— Come, the truth, now!
CYRANO (*rises*):                            That Silenus,
    Who cannot hold his belly in his arms,
    Still dreams of being sweetly dangerous
    Among the women—sighs and languishes,
    Making sheeps' eyes out of his great frog's face—
    I hate him ever since one day he dared
    Smile upon—
                    Oh, my friend, I seemed to see
    Over some flower a great snail crawling!
LE BRET (*amazed*):                            How,
    What? Is it possible?—
CYRANO (*with a bitter smile*): For me to love? . . .
    (*Changing his tone; seriously*)
    I love.
LE BRET:   May I know? You have never said—
CYRANO:  Whom I love? Think a moment. Think of me—
    Me, whom the plainest woman would despise—
    Me, with this nose of mine that marches on
    Before me by a quarter of an hour!
    Whom should I love? Why—of course—it must be
    The woman in the world most beautiful.
LE BRET: Most beautiful?
CYRANO:                    In all this world—most sweet;
    Also most wise; most witty; and most fair!
LE BRET: Who and what is this woman?
CYRANO:                            Dangerous
    Mortally, without meaning; exquisite
    Without imagining. Nature's own snare
    To allure manhood. A white rose wherein
    Love lies in ambush for his natural prey.

Who knows her smile has known a perfect thing.
She creates grace in her own image, brings
Heaven to earth in one movement of her hand—
Nor thou, O Venus! balancing thy shell
Over the Mediterranean blue, nor thou,
Diana! marching through broad, blossoming woods,
Art so divine as when she mounts her chair,
And goes abroad through Paris!

LE BRET:                                    Oh, well—of course,
   That makes everything clear!

CYRANO:                              Transparently.

LE BRET: Madeleine Robin—your cousin?

CYRANO:                                    Yes; Roxane.

LE BRET:
   And why not? If you love her, tell her so!
   You have covered yourself with glory in her eyes
   This very day.

CYRANO:                              My old friend—look at me,
   And tell me how much hope remains for me
   With this protuberance! Oh I have no more
   Illusions! Now and then—bah! I may grow
   Tender, walking alone in the blue cool
   Of evening, through some garden fresh with
        flowers
   After the benediction of the rain;
   My poor big devil of a nose inhales
   April . . . and so I follow with my eyes
   Where some boy, with a girl upon his arm,
   Passes a patch of silver . . . and I feel
   Somehow, I wish I had a woman too,
   Walking with little steps under the moon,
   And holding my arm so, and smiling. Then
   I dream—and I forget. . . .
                              And then I see
   The shadow of my profile on the wall!

LE BRET: My friend! . . .

CYRANO: My friend, I have my bitter days,
Knowing myself so ugly, so alone.
Sometimes—

LE BRET: You weep?

CYRANO (*quickly*): Oh, not that ever! No,
That would be too grotesque—tears trickling down
All the long way along this nose of mine?
I will not so profane the dignity
Of sorrow. Never any tears for me!
Why, there is nothing more sublime than tears,
Nothing!—Shall I make them ridiculous
In my poor person?

LE BRET: Love's no more than chance!

CYRANO:
No. I love Cleopatra; do I appear
Cæsar? I adore Beatrice; have I
The look of Dante?

LE BRET: But your wit—your courage—
Why, that poor child who offered you just now
Your dinner! She—you saw with your own eyes,
Her eyes did not avoid you.

CYRANO: That is true . . .

LE BRET:
Well then! Roxane herself, watching your duel,
Paler than—

CYRANO: Pale?—

LE BRET: Her lips parted, her hand
Thus, at her breast— I saw it! Speak to her,
Speak, man!

CYRANO: Through my nose? She might laugh at me;
That is the one thing in this world I fear!

THE PORTER (*followed by* THE DUENNA, *approaches* CYRANO *respectfully*):
A lady asking for Monsieur.

CYRANO:                    Mon dieu . . .
    Her Duenna!—
THE DUENNA (*a sweeping curtsey*):
                    Monsieur . . .
                                   A message for you:
    From our good cousin we desire to know
    When and where we may see him privately.
CYRANO (*amazed*): To see me?
THE DUENNA (*an elaborate reverence*):
                              To see you. We have certain things
    To tell you.
CYRANO:         Certain—
THE DUENNA:            Things.
CYRANO (*trembling*):         Mon dieu! . . .
THE DUENNA:                              We go
    To-morrow, at the first flush of the dawn,
    To hear Mass at St. Roch. Then afterwards,
    Where can we meet and talk a little?
CYRANO (*catching* LE BRET's *arm*):        Where?—
    I— Ah, mon dieu! . . . mon dieu! . . .
THE DUENNA:                         Well?
CYRANO:                          I am thinking . . .
THE DUENNA: And you think?
CYRANO:            I . . . The shop of Ragueneau . . .
    Ragueneau—pastrycook . . .
THE DUENNA:                Who dwells?—
CYRANO:                          Mon dieu! . . .
    Oh, yes . . . Ah, mon dieu! . . . Rue St.-Honoré.
THE DUENNA:
    We are agreed. Remember—seven o'clock.
    Until then—
CYRANO:      I'll be there.
    (THE DUENNA *goes out*)
CYRANO (*falls into the arms of* LE BRET):
                    Me . . . to see me! . . .

LE BRET: You are not quite so gloomy.

CYRANO:                          After all,
She knows that I exist—no matter why!

LE BRET: So now, you are going to be happy.

CYRANO:                          Now! . . .
(*beside himself*)
I—I am going to be a storm—a flame—
I need to fight whole armies all alone;
I have ten hearts; I have a hundred arms; I feel
Too strong to war with mortals—
(*he shouts at the top of his voice*)

                          BRING ME GIANTS!
(*A moment since, the shadows of the comedians have been
visible moving and posturing upon the stage. The violins have
taken their places*)

A VOICE (*from the stage*):
Hey—pst—less noise! We are rehearsing here!

CYRANO (*laughs*): We are going.
(*He turns upstage. Through the street door enter* CUIGY,
BRISSAILLE, *and a number of officers, supporting* LIGNIÈRE,
*who is now thoroughly drunk*)

CUIGY:                          Cyrano!

CYRANO:                          What is it?

CUIGY:                                    Here—
Here's your stray lamb!

CYRANO (*recognizes* LIGNIÈRE):
                    Lignière!—What's wrong with him?

CUIGY: He wants you.

BRISSAILLE:          He's afraid to go home.

CYRANO:                          Why?

LIGNIÈRE (*showing a crumpled scrap of paper and speaking with
the elaborate logic of profound intoxication*):
This letter—hundred against one—that's me—
I'm the one—all because of little song—
Good song— Hundred men, waiting, understand?

Porte de Nesle—way home— Might be dangerous—
Would you permit me spend the night with you?
CYRANO: A hundred—is that all? You are going home!
LIGNIÈRE (*astonished*): Why—
CYRANO (*in a voice of thunder, indicating the lighted lantern which* THE PORTER *holds up curiously as he regards the scene*):

Take that lantern!
(LIGNIÈRE *precipitately seizes the lantern*)

Forward march! I say
I'll be the man to-night that sees you home.
(*To the officers*)
You others follow—I want an audience!
CUIGY: A hundred against one—
CYRANO:                              Those are the odds
To-night!
(*The comedians in their costumes are descending from the stage and joining the group*)
LE BRET:      But why help this—
CYRANO:                              There goes Le Bret
Growling!
LE BRET:      —This drunkard here?
CYRANO (*his hand on* LE BRET'S *shoulder*):

Because this drunkard—
This tun of sack, this butt of Burgundy—
Once in his life has done one lovely thing:
After the Mass, according to the form,
He saw, one day, the lady of his heart
Take holy water for a blessing. So
This one, who shudders at a drop of rain,
This fellow here—runs headlong to the font
Bends down and drinks it dry!
A COMEDIENNE:                         I say that was
A pretty thought!
CYRANO:               Ah, was it not?

THE COMEDIENNE (*to the others*):        But why
   Against one poor poet, a hundred men?
CYRANO: March!                                (*to the officers*)
              And you gentlemen, remember now,
   No rescue— Let me fight alone.
A SECOND COMEDIENNE (*jumps down from the stage*):
                                        Come on!
   I'm going to watch—
CYRANO:                Come along!
ANOTHER COMEDIENNE (*jumps down, speaks to a comedian
   costumed as an old man*):              You, Cassandre?
CYRANO:
   Come all of you—the Doctor, Isabelle,
   Léandre—the whole company—a swarm
   Of murmuring, golden bees—we'll parody
   Italian farce and Tragedy-of-Blood;
   Ribbons for banners, masks for blazonry,
   And tambourines to be our rolling drums!
ALL THE WOMEN (*jumping for joy*):
   Bravo!—My hood— My cloak— Hurry!
JODELET (*mock heroic*):                    Lead on!—
CYRANO (*to the violins*):
   You violins—play us an overture—
   (*The violins join the procession which is forming. The lighted
   candles are snatched from the stage and distributed; it
   becomes a torchlight procession*)
   Bravo!—Officers— Ladies in costume—
   And twenty paces in advance. . . .
                          (*he takes his station as he speaks*)
                          Myself,
   Alone, with glory fluttering over me,
   Alone as Lucifer at war with heaven!
   Remember—no one lifts a hand to help—
   Ready there? One . . . two . . . three! Porter, the
      doors! . . .

(THE PORTER *flings wide the great doors. We see in the dim moonlight a corner of old Paris, purple and picturesque*)
Look—Paris dreams—nocturnal, nebulous,
Under blue moonbeams hung from wall to wall—
Nature's own setting for the scene we play!—
Yonder, behind her veil of mist, the Seine,
Like a mysterious and magic mirror
Trembles—

       And you shall see what you shall see!

ALL: To the Porte de Nesle!

CYRANO (*erect upon the threshold*):

       To the Porte de Nesle!

(*He turns back for a moment to the* COMEDIENNE)
Did you not ask, my dear, why against one
Singer they send a hundred swords?

       (*Quietly, drawing his own sword*)

       Because
They know this one man for a friend of mine!

*He goes out. The procession follows:* LIGNIÈRE *zigzagging at its head, then the comediennes on the arms of the officers, then the comedians, leaping and dancing as they go. It vanishes into the night to the music of the violins, illuminated by the flickering glimmer of the candles.*


CURTAIN

# ACT II

## THE BAKERY OF THE POETS

THE SHOP OF RAGUENEAU, *Baker and Pastrycook: a spacious affair at the corner of the Rue St.-Honoré and the Rue de l' Arbre Sec. The street, seen vaguely through the glass panes in the door at the back, is gray in the first light of dawn.*
*In the foreground, at the left, a counter is surmounted by a canopy of wrought iron from which are hanging ducks, geese, and white peacocks. Great crockery jars hold bouquets of common flowers, yellow sunflowers in particular. On the same side farther back, a huge fireplace; in front of it, between great andirons, of which each one supports a little saucepan, roast fowls revolve and weep into their dripping-pans. To the right at the first entrance, a door. Beyond it, second entrance, a staircase leads up to a little dining-room under the eaves, its interior visible through open shutters. A table is set there and a tiny Flemish candlestick is lighted; there one may retire to eat and drink in private. A wooden gallery, extending from the head of the stairway, seems to lead to other little dining-rooms.*
*In the centre of the shop, an iron ring hangs by a rope over a pulley so that it can be raised or lowered; adorned with game of various kinds hung from it by hooks, it has the appearance of a sort of gastronomic chandelier.*
*In the shadow under the staircase, ovens are glowing. The spits revolve; the copper pots and pans gleam ruddily. Pastries in pyramids. Hams hanging from the rafters. The morning baking is in progress: a bustle of tall cooks and timid scullions and scurrying apprentices; a blossoming of white caps adorned with cock's*

43

*feathers or the wings of guinea fowl. On wicker trays or on great metal platters they bring in rows of pastries and fancy dishes of various kinds.*

*Tables are covered with trays of cakes and rolls; others with chairs placed about them are set for guests.*

*One little table in a corner disappears under a heap of papers. At the Curtain Rise* RAGUENEAU *is seated there. He is writing poetry.*

A PASTRYCOOK (*brings in a dish*): Fruits en gelée!

SECOND PASTRYCOOK (*brings dish*):                    Custard!

THIRD PASTRYCOOK (*brings roast peacock ornamented with feathers*): Peacock rôti!

FOURTH PASTRYCOOK (*brings tray of cakes*):
                                    Cakes and confections!

FIFTH PASTRYCOOK (*brings earthen dish*): Beef en casserole!

RAGUENEAU (*raises his head; returns to mere earth*):
        Over the coppers of my kitchen flows
        The frosted-silver dawn. Silence awhile
        The god who sings within thee, Ragueneau!
        Lay down the lute—the oven calls for thee!
                        (*Rises; goes to one of the cooks*)
        Here's a hiatus in your sauce; fill up
        The measure.

THE COOK:        How much?

RAGUENEAU (*measures on his finger*):                    One more dactyl.

THE COOK: Huh? . . .

FIRST PASTRYCOOK:    Rolls!

SECOND PASTRYCOOK:        Roulades!

RAGUENEAU (*before the fireplace*):
                            Veil, O Muse, thy virgin eyes
        From the lewd gleam of these terrestrial fires!
                                (*To First Pastrycook*)
        Your rolls lack balance. Here's the proper form—
        An equal hemistich on either side,
        And the caesura in between.
                        (*To another, pointing out an unfinished pie*)

                              Your house
Of crust should have a roof upon it.
(*To another, who is seated on the hearth, placing poultry on a
spit*)                              And you—
Along the interminable spit, arrange
The modest pullet and the lordly Turk
Alternately, my son—as great Malherbe
Alternates male and female rhymes. Remember,
A couplet, or a roast, should be well turned.

AN APPRENTICE (*advances with a dish covered by a napkin*):
    Master, I thought of you when I designed
    This, hoping it might please you.

RAGUENEAU:                        Ah! A lyre—

THE APPRENTICE:                              In puff-paste—

RAGUENEAU: And the jewels—candied fruit!

THE APPRENTICE:              And the strings, barley-sugar!

RAGUENEAU (*gives him money*):      Go and drink
    My health.                              (LISE *enters*)
                St!—My wife— Circulate, and hide
    That money!    (*Shows the lyre to* LISE, *with a languid air*)
                Graceful—yes?

LISE:                        Ridiculous!
    (*She places on the counter a pile of paper bags*)

RAGUENEAU: Paper bags? Thank you . . . (*he looks at them*)
                              Ciel! My manuscripts!
    The sacred verses of my poets—rent
    Asunder, limb from limb—butchered to make
    Base packages of pastry! Ah, you are one
    Of those insane Bacchantes who destroyed
    Orpheus!

LISE:          Your dirty poets left them here
    To pay for eating half our stock-in-trade:
    We ought to make some profit out of them!

RAGUENEAU: Ant! Would you blame the locust for his song?

LISE: I blame the locust for his appetite!

LISE: There used to be a time—before you had
Your hungry friends—you never called me Ants—
No, nor Bacchantes!
RAGUENEAU:              What a way to use
Poetry!
LISE:        Well, what is the use of it?
RAGUENEAU:
But, my dear girl, what would you do with prose?
Well, dears?                        (*Two children enter*)
A CHILD:        Three little patties.
RAGUENEAU (*serves them*):          There we are!
All hot and brown.
THE CHILD:              Would you mind wrapping them?
RAGUENEAU: One of my paper bags! . . .
                                        Oh, certainly.
(*Reads from the bag, as he is about to wrap the patties in it*)
"Ulysses, when he left Penelope"—
Not that one!                    (*Takes another bag; reads*)
        "Phoebus, golden-crowned"—
                                Not that one.
LISE: Well? They are waiting!
RAGUENEAU:              Very well, very well!—
The Sonnet to Phyllis . . .
                        Yet—it does seem hard . . .
LISE: Made up your mind—at last! Mph!—Jack-o'-Dreams!
RAGUENEAU (*as her back is turned, calls back the children, who
are already at the door*):
Pst!—Children— Give me back the bag. Instead
Of three patties, you shall have six of them!
(*Makes the exchange. The children go out. He reads from the
bag, as he smooths it out tenderly*)
"Phyllis"—
        A spot of butter on her name!—
"Phyllis"—
CYRANO (*enters hurriedly*): What is the time?

RAGUENEAU:                                   Six o'clock.

CYRANO:                                            One
Hour more . . .

RAGUENEAU:          Felicitations!

CYRANO:                                And for what?

RAGUENEAU: Your victory! I saw it all—

CYRANO:                                Which one?

RAGUENEAU: At the Hôtel de Bourgogne.

CYRANO:                                        Oh—the duel!

RAGUENEAU: The duel in Rhyme!

LISE:                        He talks of nothing else.

CYRANO: Nonsense!

RAGUENEAU (*fencing and foining with a spit, which he snatches up from the hearth*):
            "Then, as I end the refrain, thrust home!"
    "Then, as I end the refrain"—
                                Gods! What a line!
    "Then, as I end"—

CYRANO:              What time now, Ragueneau?

RAGUENEAU (*petrified at the full extent of a lunge, while he looks at the clock*): Five after six— (*recovers*)
                        "—thrust home!"
                                A Ballade, too!

LISE (*to CYRANO, who in passing has mechanically shaken hands with her*): Your hand—what have you done?

CYRANO:                    Oh, my hand?—Nothing.

RAGUENEAU: What danger now—

CYRANO:                    No danger.

LISE:                              I believe
He is lying.

CYRANO:      Why? Was I looking down my nose?
That must have been a devil of a lie!
                        (*Changing his tone; to* RAGUENEAU)
I expect someone. Leave us here alone,
When the time comes.

RAGUENEAU:                    How can I? In a moment,
   My poets will be here.
LISE:                         To break their . . . fast!
CYRANO:
   Take them away, then, when I give the sign.
   —What time?
RAGUENEAU:          Ten minutes past.
CYRANO:                              Have you a pen?
RAGUENEAU (*offers him a pen*): An eagle's feather!
A MUSKETEER (*enters, and speaks to* LISE *in a stentorian voice*):
   Greeting!
CYRANO (*to* RAGUENEAU): Who is this?
RAGUENEAU:
   My wife's friend. A terrific warrior,
   So he says.
CYRANO:          Ah— I see.
   (*Takes up the pen; waves* RAGUENEAU *away*)
               Only to write—
   To fold— To give it to her—and to go . . .
                 (*throws down the pen*)
   Coward! And yet—the Devil take my soul
   If I dare speak one word to her . . .
   (*To* RAGUENEAU)                    What time now?
RAGUENEAU: A quarter past six.
CYRANO (*striking his breast*):      —One little word
   Of all the many thousand I have here!
   Whereas in writing . . .          (*takes up the pen*)
                Come, I'll write to her
   That letter I have written on my heart,
   Torn up, and written over many times—
   So many times . . . that all I have to do
   Is to remember, and to write it down.
   (*He writes. Through the glass of the door appear vague and hesitating shadows. The poets enter, clothed in rusty black and spotted with mud*)

LISE (*to* RAGUENEAU): Here come your scarecrows!

FIRST POET:                                    Comrade!

SECOND POET (*takes both* RAGUENEAU'S *hands*):
  My dear brother!

THIRD POET (*sniffing*):
  O Lord of Roasts, how sweet thy dwellings are!

FOURTH POET: Phoebus Apollo of the Silver Spoon!

FIFTH POET: Cupid of Cookery!

RAGUENEAU (*surrounded, embraced, beaten on the back*):
                                    These geniuses,
  They put one at one's ease!

FIRST POET:                      We were delayed
  By the crowd at the Porte de Nesle.

SECOND POET:                      .      Dead men
  All scarred and gory, scattered on the stones,
  Villainous-looking scoundrels—eight of them.

CYRANO (*looks up an instant*): Eight? I thought only seven—

RAGUENEAU:                              Do you know
  The hero of this hecatomb?

CYRANO:                      I? . . . No.

LISE (*to* THE MUSKETEER):              Do you?

THE MUSKETEER: Hmm—perhaps!

FIRST POET:                      They say one man alone
  Put to flight all this crowd.

SECOND POET:                  Everywhere lay
  Swords, daggers, pikes, bludgeons—

CYRANO (*writing*):                      "Your eyes . . ."

THIRD POET:                                    As far
  As the Quai des Orfevres, hats and cloaks—

FIRST POET: Why, that man must have been the devil!

CYRANO:                              "Your lips . . ."

FIRST POET:
  Some savage monster might have done this thing!

CYRANO: "Looking upon you, I grow faint with fear . . ."

SECOND POET: What have you written lately, Ragueneau?

CYRANO: "Your Friend—Who loves you . . ."

So. No signature;
I'll give it to her myself.

RAGUENEAU:                     A Recipe   In Rhyme.

THIRD POET:   Read us your rhymes!

FOURTH POET:                     Here's a brioche
Cocking its hat at me.          (*He bites off the top of it*)

FIRST POET:          Look how those buns
Follow the hungry poet with their eyes—
Those almond eyes!

SECOND POET:          We are listening—

THIRD POET:                     See this cream-puff—
Fat little baby, drooling while it smiles!

SECOND POET (*nibbling at the pastry lyre*):
For the first time, the lyre is my support.

RAGUENEAU (*coughs, adjusts his cap, strikes an attitude*):
A Recipe in Rhyme—

SECOND POET (*gives* FIRST POET *a dig with his elbow*):
Your breakfast?

FIRST POET:                     Dinner!

RAGUENEAU (*declaims*):
A Recipe for Making Almond Tarts

Beat your eggs, the yolk and white,
     Very light;
Mingle with their creamy fluff
     Drops of lime-juice, cool and green;
          Then pour in
Milk of Almonds, just enough.

Dainty patty-pans, embraced
     In puff-paste—
Have these ready within reach;
     With your thumb and finger, pinch
          Half an inch
Up around the edge of each—

                   Into these, a score or more,
                        Slowly pour
              All your store of custard; so
                Take them, bake them golden-brown—
                        Now sit down! . . .
                   Almond tartlets, Ragueneau!


THE POETS: Delicious! Melting!
A POET (*chokes*):              Humph!
CYRANO (*to* RAGUENEAU):              Do you not see
     Those fellows fattening themselves?—
RAGUENEAU:                        I know.
     I would not look—it might embarrass them—
     You see, I love a friendly audience.
     Besides—another vanity—I am pleased
     When they enjoy my cooking.
CYRANO (*slaps him on the back*):     Be off with you!—
     (RAGUENEAU *goes upstage*)
     Good little soul!                    (*Calls to* LISE)
                   Madame!—
     (*She leaves* THE MUSKETEER *and comes down to him*)
                             This musketeer—
     He is making love to you?
LISE (*haughtily*):              If any man
     Offends my virtue—all I have to do
     Is look at him—once!
CYRANO (*looks at her gravely; she drops her eyes*):
                        I do not find
     Those eyes of yours unconquerable.
LISE (*panting*):                   —Ah!
CYRANO (*raising his voice a little*):
     Now listen— I am fond of Ragueneau;
     I allow no one—do you understand?—
     To . . . take his name in vain!
LISE:                        You think—

CYRANO (*ironic emphasis*):                              I think
    I interrupt you.
    (*He salutes* THE MUSKETEER, *who has heard without daring
    to resent the warning.* LISE *goes to* THE MUSKETEER *as he
    returns* CYRANO'S *salute*)
LISE:                              You—you swallow that?—
    You ought to have pulled his nose!
THE MUSKETEER:                    His nose?—His nose! . . .
    (*He goes out hurriedly.* ROXANE *and* THE DUENNA *appear
    outside the door*)
CYRANO (*nods to* RAGUENEAU): Pst!—
RAGUENEAU (*to the Poets*):                    Come inside—
CYRANO (*impatient*): Pst! . . . Pst! . . .
RAGUENEAU:                              We shall be more
    Comfortable . . .        (*he leads the Poets into inner room*)
FIRST POET:              The cakes!
SECOND POET:                    Bring them along!
    (*They go out*)
CYRANO:
    If I can see the faintest spark of hope,
    Then—                    (*throws door open—bows*)
        Welcome!
    (ROXANE *enters, followed by* THE DUENNA, *whom* CYRANO
    *detains*)
                Pardon me—one word—
THE DUENNA:                              Take two.
CYRANO: Have you a good digestion?
THE DUENNA:                    Wonderful!
CYRANO:
    Good. Here are two sonnets, by Benserade—
THE DUENNA: Euh?
CYRANO:              Which I fill for you with éclairs.
THE DUENNA:                              Ooo!
CYRANO: Do you like cream-puffs?
THE DUENNA:              Only with whipped cream.

CYRANO:
> Here are three . . . six—embosomed in a poem
> By Saint-Amant. This ode of Chapelin
> Looks deep enough to hold—a jelly roll.
> —Do you love Nature?

THE DUENNA: Mad about it.

CYRANO: Then
> Go out and eat these in the street. Do not
> Return—

THE DUENNA: Oh, but—

CYRANO: Until you finish them.
> (*Down to* ROXANE)
> Blessed above all others be the hour
> When you remembered to remember me,
> And came to tell me . . . what?

ROXANE (*takes off her mask*): First let me thank you
> Because . . . That man . . . that creature, whom
>     your sword
> Made sport of yesterday— His patron, one—

CYRANO: De Guiche?—

ROXANE: —who thinks himself in love with me
> Would have forced that man upon me for—
>     a husband—

CYRANO:
> I understand—so much the better then!
> I fought, not for my nose, but your bright eyes.

ROXANE:
> And then, to tell you—but before I can
> Tell you— Are you, I wonder, still the same
> Big brother—almost—that you used to be
> When we were children, playing by the pond
> In the old garden down there—

CYRANO: I remember—
> Every summer you came to Bergerac! . . .

ROXANE: You used to make swords out of bulrushes—

CYRANO: Your dandelion-dolls with golden hair—
ROXANE: And those green plums—
CYRANO:                     And those black mulberries—
ROXANE: In those days, you did everything I wished!
CYRANO: Roxane, in short skirts, was called Madeleine.
ROXANE: Was I pretty?
CYRANO:               Oh—not too plain!
ROXANE:                                   Sometimes
    When you had hurt your hand you used to come
    Running to me—and I would be your mother,
    And say— Oh, in a very grown-up voice:
    (*she takes his hand*)
    "Now, what have you been doing to yourself?
    Let me see—"                    (*she sees the hand—starts*)
              Oh!—
                  Wait— I said, "Let me see!"
    Still—at your age! How did you do that?
CYRANO:                                   Playing
    With the big boys, down by the Porte de Nesle.
ROXANE (*sits at a table and wets her handkerchief in a glass of
    water*): Come here to me.
CYRANO:                   —Such a wise little mother!
ROXANE:
    And tell me, while I wash this blood away,
    How many you—played with?
CYRANO:                         Oh, about a hundred.
ROXANE: Tell me.
CYRANO:         No. Let me go. Tell me what you
    Were going to tell me—if you dared?
ROXANE (*still holding his hand*):         I think
    I do dare—now. It seems like long ago
    When I could tell you things. Yes—I dare . . .
          Listen:
    I . . . love someone.
CYRANO:                 Ah! . . .

ROXANE: Someone who does not know.

CYRANO: Ah! . . .

ROXANE: At least—not yet.

CYRANO: Ah! . . .

ROXANE: But he will know
Some day.

CYRANO: Ah! . . .

ROXANE: A big boy who loves me too,
And is afraid of me, and keeps away,
And never says one word.

CYRANO: Ah! . . .

ROXANE: Let me have
Your hand a moment—why how hot it is!—
I know. I see him trying . . .

CYRANO: Ah! . . .

ROXANE: There now!
Is that better?—
(*She finishes bandaging the hand with her handkerchief*)
Besides—only to think—
(This is a secret.) He is a soldier too,
In your own regiment—

CYRANO: Ah! . . .

ROXANE: Yes, in the Guards,
Your company too.

CYRANO: Ah! . . .

ROXANE: And such a man!—
He is proud—noble—young—brave—beautiful—

CYRANO (*turns pale; rises*): Beautiful!—

ROXANE: What's the matter?

CYRANO (*smiling*): Nothing—this—
My sore hand!

ROXANE: Well, I love him. That is all.
Oh—and I never saw him anywhere
Except the *Comedie*.

CYRANO: You have never spoken?—

ROXANE: Only our eyes . . .

CYRANO                    Why, then— How do you know?—

ROXANE:

　　People talk about people; and I hear
　　Things . . . and I know.

CYRANO:                    You say he is in the Guards:
　　His name?

ROXANE:        Baron Christian de Neuvillette.

CYRANO: He is not in the Guards.

ROXANE:                    Yes. Since this morning.
　　Captain Carbon de Castel-Jaloux.

CYRANO:                    So soon! . . .
　　So soon we lose our hearts!—

　　　　　　　　　　　　But, my dear child,—

THE DUENNA (*opens the door*):

　　I have eaten the cakes, Monsieur de Bergerac!

CYRANO:

　　Good! Now go out and read the poetry!

　　　　　　　　　　　(THE DUENNA *disappears*)
　　—But, my dear child! You, who love only words,
　　Wit, the grand manner— Why, for all you know,
　　The man may be a savage, or a fool.

ROXANE: His curls are like a hero's from D'Urfé.

CYRANO: His mind may be as curly as his hair.

ROXANE: Not with such eyes. I read his soul in them.

CYRANO:

　　Yes, all our souls are written in our eyes!
　　But—if he be a bungler?

ROXANE:                    Then I shall die—
　　There!

CYRANO (*after a pause*):

　　　　　And you brought me here to tell me this?
　　I do not yet quite understand, Madame,
　　The reason for your confidence.

ROXANE:                              They say
    That in your company— It frightens me—
    You are all Gascons . . .
CYRANO:                        And we pick a quarrel
    With any flat-foot who intrudes himself,
    Whose blood is not pure Gascon like our own?
    Is this what you have heard?
ROXANE:                        I am so afraid
    For him!
CYRANO (*between his teeth*): Not without reason!—
ROXANE:                              And I thought
    You . . . You were so brave, so invincible
    Yesterday, against all those brutes!—If you,
    Whom they all fear—
CYRANO:                    Oh well— I will defend
    Your little Baron.
ROXANE:              Will you? Just for me?
    Because I have always been—your friend!
CYRANO:                                    Of course . . .
ROXANE: Will you be *his* friend?
CYRANO:                        I will be his friend.
ROXANE: And never let him fight a duel?
CYRANO:                              No—never.
ROXANE:
    Oh, but you are a darling!—I must go—
    You never told me about last night— Why,
    You must have been a hero! Have him write
    And tell me all about it—will you?
CYRANO:                                Of course . . .
ROXANE (*kisses her hand*):
    I always did love you!—A hundred men
    Against one— Well. . . . Adieu. We are great
        friends,
    Are we not?
CYRANO:      Of course . . .
    3

ROXANE:                              He *must* write to me—
A hundred— You shall tell me the whole story
Some day, when I have time. A hundred men—
What courage!

CYRANO (*salutes as she goes out*):
                    Oh . . . I have done better since!

(*The door closes after her.* CYRANO *remains motionless, his eyes on the ground. Pause. The other door opens;* RAGUENEAU *puts in his head*)

RAGUENEAU: May I come in?

CYRANO (*without moving*):     Yes . . .

(RAGUENEAU *and his friends re-enter. At the same time,* CARBON DE CASTEL-JALOUX *appears at the street door in uniform as Captain of the Guards; recognizes* CYRANO *with a sweeping gesture*)

CARBON:                          Here he is!—Our hero!

CYRANO (*raises his head and salutes*): Our Captain!

CARBON:                      We know! All our company
Are here—

CYRANO (*recoils*): No—

CARBON:          Come! They are waiting for you.

CYRANO:                                      No!

CARBON (*tries to lead him out*):
Only across the street— Come!

CYRANO:                        Please—

CARBON (*goes to the door and shouts in a voice of thunder*):
                                Our champion
Refuses! He is not feeling well to-day!

A VOICE OUTSIDE: Ah! Sandious!

(*Noise outside of swords and trampling feet approaching*)

CARBON:                      Here they come now!

THE CADETS (*entering the shop*):          Mille dious!—
Mordious!—Capdedious!—Pocapdedious!

RAGUENEAU (*in astonishment*):              Gentlemen—
You are all Gascons?

THE CADETS: All!

FIRST CADET (*to* CYRANO): Bravo!

CYRANO: Baron!

ANOTHER CADET (*takes both his hands*): Vivat!

CYRANO: Baron!

THIRD CADET: Come to my arms!

CYRANO: Baron!

OTHERS: To mine!—To mine!—

CYRANO: Baron . . . Baron . . . Have mercy—

RAGUENEAU: You are all Barons too?

THE CADETS: *Are* we?

RAGUENEAU: Are they? . . .

FIRST CADET: Our coronets would star the midnight sky!

LE BRET (*enters; hurries to* CYRANO):
　　The whole town's looking for you! Raving mad—
　　A triumph! Those who saw the fight—

CYRANO: I hope
　　You have not told them where I—

LE BRET (*rubbing his hands*): Certainly
　　I told them!

CITIZEN (*enters, followed by a group*):
　　　　Listen! Shut the door!—Here comes
　　All Paris!
　　(*The street outside fills with a shouting crowd. Chairs and
　　carriages stop at the door*)

LE BRET (*aside to* CYRANO, *smiling*): And Roxane?

CYRANO (*quickly*): Hush!

THE CROWD OUTSIDE: Cyrano!
　　(*A mob bursts into the shop. Shouts, acclamations, general
　　disturbance*)

RAGUENEAU (*standing on a table*):
　　My shop invaded— They'll break everything—
　　Glorious!

SEVERAL MEN (*crowding about* CYRANO):
　　　　My friend! . . . My friend! . . .

CYRANO:                                          Why, yesterday
    I did not have so many friends!
LE BRET:                               Success
    At last!
A MARQUIS (*runs to* CYRANO, *with outstretched hands*):
                My dear—really!—
CYRANO (*coldly*):              So? And how long
    Have I been dear to you?
ANOTHER MARQUIS:           One moment—pray!
    I have two ladies in my carriage here;
    Let me present you—
CYRANO:                    Certainly! And first,
    Who will present you, sir,—to me?
LE BRET (*astounded*):                 Why, what
    The devil?—
CYRANO:         Hush!
A MAN OF LETTERS (*with a portfolio*):
                    May I have the details? . . .
CYRANO: You may not.
LE BRET (*plucking* CYRANO'S *sleeve*):
                    Theophraste Renaudot!—Editor
    Of the *Gazette*—your reputation! . . .
CYRANO:                               No!
A POET (*advances*): Monsieur—
CYRANO:               Well?
THE POET:              Your full name? I will compose
    A pentacrostic—
ANOTHER:         Monsieur—
CYRANO:                     That will do!
    (*Movement. The crowd arranges itself.* DE GUICHE
    *appears, escorted by* CUIGY, BRISSAILLE, *and the other
    officers who were with* CYRANO *at the close of the First
    Act*)
CUIGY (*goes to* CYRANO): Monsieur de Guiche!—
    (*Murmur. Everyone moves*)

A message from the Marshal
De Gassion—

DE GUICHE (*saluting* CYRANO):     Who wishes to express
Through me his admiration. He has heard
Of your affair—

THE CROWD:     Bravo!

CYRANO (*bowing*):     The Marshal speaks
As an authority.

DE GUICHE:     He said just now
The story would have been incredible
Were it not for the witness—

CUIGY:     Of our eyes!

LE BRET (*aside to* CYRANO): What is it?

CYRANO:     Hush!—

LE BRET:     Something is wrong with you;
Are you in pain?

CYRANO (*recovering himself*):
    In pain? Before this crowd?
(*His moustache bristles. He throws out his chest*)
I? In pain? You shall see!

DE GUICHE (*to whom* CUIGY *has been whispering*):
    Your name is known
Already as a soldier. You are one
Of those wild Gascons, are you not?

CYRANO:     The Guards,
Yes. A Cadet.

A CADET (*in a voice of thunder*): One of ourselves!

DE GUICHE:     Ah! So—
Then all these gentlemen with the haughty air,
These are the famous—

CARBON:     Cyrano!

CYRANO:     Captain?

CARBON:
Our troop being all present, be so kind
As to present them to the Comte de Guiche!

CYRANO (*with a gesture presenting the Cadets to* DE GUICHE, *declaims*):

> The Cadets of Gascoyne—the defenders
>> Of Carbon de Castel-Jaloux:
> Free fighters, free lovers, free spenders—
> The Cadets of Gascoyne—the defenders
> Of old homes, old names, and old splendours—
>> A proud and a pestilent crew!
> The Cadets of Gascoyne, the defenders
>> Of Carbon de Castel-Jaloux.
>
> Hawk-eyed, they stare down all contenders—
>> The wolf bares his fangs as they do—
> Make way there, you fat money-lenders!
> (Hawk-eyed, they stare down all contenders)
> Old boots that have been to the menders,
>> Old cloaks that are worn through and through—
> Hawk-eyed, they stare down all contenders—
>> The wolf bares his fangs as they do!
>
> Skull-breakers they are, and sword-benders;
>> Red blood is their favourite brew;
> Hot haters and loyal befrienders,
> Skull-breakers they are, and sword-benders.
> Wherever a quarrel engenders,
>> They're ready and waiting for you!
> Skull-breakers they are, and sword-benders;
>> Red blood is their favourite brew!
>
> Behold them, our Gascon defenders
>> Who win every woman they woo!
> There's never a dame but surrenders—
> Behold them, our Gascon defenders!
> Young wives who are clever pretenders—
>> Old husbands who house the cuckoo—
> Behold them—our Gascon defenders
>> Who win every woman they woo!

DE GUICHE (*languidly, sitting in a chair*):
    Poets are fashionable nowadays
    To have about one. Would you care to join
    My following?
CYRANO:          No, sir. I do not follow.
DE GUICHE:
    Your duel yesterday amused my uncle
    The Cardinal. I might help you there.
LE BRET:                 Grand Dieu!
DE GUICHE: I suppose you have written a tragedy—
    They all have.
LE BRET (*aside to* CYRANO):
           Now at last you'll have it played—
    Your "Agrippine!"
DE GUICHE:        Why not? Take it to him.
CYRANO (*tempted*): Really—
DE GUICHE:          He is himself a dramatist;
    Let him rewrite a few lines here and there,
    And he'll approve the rest.
CYRANO (*his face falls again*):    Impossible.
    My blood curdles to think of altering
    One comma.
DE GUICHE:      Ah, but when he likes a thing
    He pays well.
CYRANO:         Yes—but not so well as I—
    When I have made a line that sings itself
    So that I love the sound of it—I pay
    Myself a hundred times.
DE GUICHE:          You are proud, my friend.
CYRANO: You have observed that?
A CADET (*enters with a drawn sword, along the whole blade of
    which is transfixed a collection of disreputable hats, their
    plumes draggled, their crowns cut and torn*):
                  Cyrano! See here—
    Look what we found this morning in the street—

The plumes dropped in their flight by those fine birds
Who showed the white feather!

CARBON:                    Spoils of the hunt—
Well mounted!

THE CROWD:        Ha-ha-ha!

CUIGY:                    Whoever hired
Those rascals, he must be an angry man
To-day!

BRISSAILLE: Who was it? Do you know?

DE GUICHE:                    Myself!—
    (*The laughter ceases*)
I hired them to do the sort of work
We do not soil our hands with—punishing
A drunken poet. . . .        (*Uncomfortable silence*)

THE CADET (*to* CYRANO):    What shall we do with them?
They ought to be preserved before they spoil—

CYRANO (*takes the sword, and in the gesture of saluting
    DE GUICHE with it, makes all the hats slide off at his
    feet*):
Sir, will you not return these to your friends?

DE GUICHE: My chair—my porters here—immediately!
    (*To* CYRANO *violently*)
—As for you, sir!—

A VOICE (*in the street*):    The chair of Monseigneur
Le Comte de Guiche!—

DE GUICHE (*who has recovered his self-control; smiling*):
                    Have you read *Don Quixote*?

CYRANO: I have—and found myself the hero.

A PORTER (*appears at the door*):            Chair
Ready!

DE GUICHE: Be so good as to read once more
The chapter of the windmills.

CYRANO (*gravely*):            Chapter Thirteen.

DE GUICHE: Windmills, remember, if you fight with them—

CYRANO: My enemies change, then, with every wind?

DE GUICHE:

    —May swing round their huge arms and cast you down
    Into the mire.

CYRANO:          Or up—among the stars!

    (DE GUICHE *goes out. We see him get into the chair. The*
    *officers follow murmuring among themselves.* LE BRET *goes*
    *up with them. The crowd goes out*)

CYRANO (*saluting with burlesque politeness, those who go out*
    *without daring to take leave of him*):

    Gentlemen. . . . Gentlemen. . . .

LE BRET (*as the door closes, comes down, shaking his clenched*
    *hands to heaven*):        You have done it now—
    You have made your fortune!

CYRANO:             There you go again,
    Growling!—

LE BRET:      At least this latest pose of yours—
    Ruining every chance that comes your way—
    Becomes exaggerated—

CYRANO:           Very well,
    Then I exaggerate!

LE BRET (*triumphantly*): Oh, you do!

CYRANO:              Yes;
    On principle. There are things in this world
    A man does well to carry to extremes.

LE BRET:

    Stop trying to be Three Musketeers in one!
    Fortune and glory—

CYRANO:          What would you have me do?
    Seek for the patronage of some great man,
    And like a creeping vine on a tall tree
    Crawl upward, where I cannot stand alone?
    No thank you! Dedicate, as others do,
    Poems to pawnbrokers? Be a buffoon
    In the vile hope of teasing out a smile
    On some cold face? No thank you! Eat a toad

    3*

For breakfast every morning? Make my knees
Callous, and cultivate a supple spine,—
Wear out my belly grovelling in the dust?
No thank you! Scratch the back of any swine
That roots up gold for me? Tickle the horns
Of Mammon with my left hand, while my right
Too proud to know his partner's business,
Takes in the fee? No thank you! Use the fire
God gave me to burn incense all day long
Under the nose of wood and stone? No thank you!
Shall I go leaping into ladies' laps
And licking fingers?—or—to change the form—
Navigating with madrigals for oars,
My sails full of the sighs of dowagers?
No thank you! Publish verses at my own
Expense? No thank you! Be the patron saint
Of a small group of literary souls
Who dine together every Tuesday? No,
I thank you! Shall I labour night and day
To build a reputation on one song,
And never write another? Shall I find
True genius only among Geniuses,
Palpitate over little paragraphs,
And struggle to insinuate my name
Into the columns of the *Mercury*?
No thank you! Calculate, scheme, be afraid,
Love more to make a visit than a poem,
Seek introductions, favours, influences?—
No thank you! No, I thank you! And again
I thank you!—But . . .

                To sing, to laugh, to dream,
To walk in my own way and be alone,
Free, with an eye to see things as they are,
A voice that means manhood—to cock my hat
Where I choose— At a word, a *Yes*, a *No*,

To fight—or write. To travel any road
Under the sun, under the stars, nor doubt
If fame or fortune lie beyond the bourne—
Never to make a line I have not heard
In my own heart; yet, with all modesty
To say: "My soul, be satisfied with flowers,
With fruit, with weeds even; but gather them
In the one garden you may call your own."
So, when I win some triumph, by some chance,
Render no share to Cæsar—in a word,
I am too proud to be a parasite,
And if my nature wants the germ that grows
Towering to heaven like the mountain pine,
Or like the oak, sheltering multitudes—
I stand, not high it may be—but alone!

LE BRET:
Alone, yes!—But why stand against the world?
What devil has possessed you now, to go
Everywhere making yourself enemies?

CYRANO:
Watching you other people making friends
Everywhere—as a dog makes friends! I mark
The manner of these canine courtesies
And think: "My friends are of a cleaner breed;
Here comes—thank God!—another enemy!"

LE BRET: But this is madness!

CYRANO:                    Method, let us say.
It is my pleasure to displease. I love
Hatred. Imagine how it feels to face
The volley of a thousand angry eyes—
The bile of envy and the froth of fear
Spattering little drops about me— You—
Good nature all around you, soft and warm—
You are like those Italians, in great cowls
Comfortable and loose— Your chin sinks down

Into the folds, your shoulders droop. But I—
The Spanish ruff I wear around my throat
Is like a ring of enemies; hard, proud,
Each point another pride, another thorn—
So that I hold myself erect perforce.
Wearing the hatred of the common herd
Haughtily, the harsh collar of Old Spain,
At once a fetter and—a halo!

LE BRET:                          Yes . . .
*(After a silence, draws* CYRANO'S *arm through his own)*
Tell this to all the world— And then to me
Say very softly that . . . She loves you not.

CYRANO *(quickly)*: Hush!
*(A moment since,* CHRISTIAN *has entered and mingled with
the Cadets, who do not offer to speak to him. Finally, he sits
down alone at a small table, where he is served by* LISE*)*

A CADET *(rises from a table upstage, his glass in his hand)*:
                          Cyrano!—Your story!

CYRANO:                          Presently . . .
*(He goes up, on the arm of* LE BRET, *talking to him.* THE
CADET *comes downstage)*

THE CADET:
The story of the combat! An example
For—
*(he stops by the table where* CHRISTIAN *is sitting)*
—this young tadpole here.

CHRISTIAN *(looks up)*:          Tadpole?

ANOTHER CADET:                          Yes, you!—
You narrow-gutted Northerner!

CHRISTIAN:                          Sir?

FIRST CADET:                          Hark ye,
Monsieur de Neuvillette: You are to know
There is a certain subject—I would say,
A certain object—never to be named
Among us: utterly unmentionable!

CHRISTIAN: And that is . . . ?
THIRD CADET (*in an awful voice*):
                    Look at me! . . .
    (*He strikes his nose three times with his finger, mysteriously*)
                                    You understand?
CHRISTIAN: Why, yes; the—
FOURTH CADET:      Sh! . . . We never speak that word—
    (*indicating* CYRANO *by a gesture*)
    To breathe it is to have to do with HIM!
FIFTH CADET (*speaks through his nose*):
    He has exterminated several
    Whose tone of voice suggested . . .
SIXTH CADET (*in a hollow tone; rising from under the table on
    all fours*):                          Would you die
    Before your time? Just mention anything
    Convex . . . or cartilaginous . . .
SEVENTH CADET (*his hand on* CHRISTIAN'S *shoulder*):
                                    One word—
    One syllable—one gesture—nay, one sneeze—
    Your handkerchief becomes your winding-sheet!
    (*Silence. In a circle around* CHRISTIAN, *arms crossed, they
    regard him expectantly*)
CHRISTIAN (*rises and goes to* CARBON, *who is conversing with an
    officer, and pretending not to see what is taking place*):
    Captain!
CARBON (*turns, and looks him over*): Sir?
CHRISTIAN:                  What is the proper thing to do
    When Gascons grow too boastful?
CARBON:                          Prove to them
    That one may be a Norman, and have courage.
    (*Turns his back*)
CHRISTIAN: I thank you.
FIRST CADET (*to* CYRANO): Come—the story!
ALL:                              The story!

CYRANO (*comes down*): Oh,
    My story? Well . . .
    (*They all draw up their stools and group themselves around him,
    eagerly.* CHRISTIAN *places himself astride of a chair, his
    arms on the back of it*)
                     I marched on, all alone
To meet those devils. Overhead, the moon
Hung like a gold watch at the fob of heaven,
Till suddenly some Angel rubbed a cloud,
As it might be his handkerchief, across
The shining crystal, and—the night came down.
No lamps in those back streets— It was so dark—
Mordious! You could not see beyond—
CHRISTIAN:                      Your nose.
    (*Silence. Every man slowly rises to his feet. They look at
      CYRANO almost with terror. He has stopped short, utterly
    astonished. Pause*)
CYRANO: Who is that man there?
A CADET (*in a low voice*):        A recruit—arrived
    This morning.
CYRANO (*takes a step toward* CHRISTIAN):
             A recruit—
CARBON (*in a low voice*):    His name is Christian
    De Neuvil—
CYRANO (*suddenly motionless*): Oh! . . .
    (*he turns pale, flushes, makes a movement as if to throw
    himself upon* CHRISTIAN)
                  I—
    (*controls himself, and goes on in a choking voice*)
                    I see. Very well,
As I was saying—       (*with a sudden burst of rage*)
             Mordious! . . .
              (*he goes on in a natural tone*)
                It grew dark,
You could not see your hand before your eyes.

I marched on, thinking how, all for the sake
Of one old souse    (*They slowly sit down, watching him*)
                    who wrote a bawdy song
Whenever he took—
CHRISTIAN:              A noseful—
(*Everyone rises.* CHRISTIAN *balances himself on two legs of his chair*)
CYRANO (*half strangled*):              —Took a notion . . .
Whenever he took a notion— For his sake,
I might antagonize some dangerous man,
One powerful enough to make me pay—
CHRISTIAN: Through the nose—
CYRANO (*wipes the sweat from his forehead*):
                    —Pay the Piper. After all,
I thought, why am I putting in my—
CHRISTIAN:                  Nose—
CYRANO:—My oar . . . Why am I putting in my oar?
The quarrel's none of mine. However—now
I am here, I may as well go through with it.
Come Gascon—do your duty!—Suddenly
A sword flashed in the dark. I caught it fair—
CHRISTIAN: On the nose—
CYRANO                  On my blade. Before I knew it,
There I was—
CHRISTIAN:        Rubbing noses—
CYRANO (*pale and smiling*):          Crossing swords
With half a score at once. I handed one—
CHRISTIAN: A nosegay—
CYRANO (*leaping at him*): Ventre-Saint-Gris! . . .
(*The Gascons tumble over each other to get a good view. Arrived in front of* CHRISTIAN, *who has not moved an inch,* CYRANO *masters himself again, and continues*)
                    He went down;
The rest gave way; I charged—
CHRISTIAN:              Nose in the air—

CYRANO: I skewered two of them—disarmed a third—
  Another lunged— Paf! And I countered—
CHRISTIAN:                                    Pif!
CYRANO (*bellowing*): TONNERRE! Out of here!—All of you!
  (*All the Cadets rush for the door*)
FIRST CADET:                            At last—
  The old lion wakes!
CYRANO:              All of you! Leave me here
  Alone with that man!
  (*The lines following are heard brokenly, in the confusion of
  getting through the door*)
SECOND CADET:          Bigre! He'll have the fellow
  Chopped into sausage—
RAGUENEAU:              Sausage?—
THIRD CADET:                      Mince-meat, then—
  One of your pies!—
RAGUENEAU:          Am I pale? You look white
  As a fresh napkin—
CARBON (*at the door*):  Come!
FOURTH CADET:              He'll never leave
  Enough of him to—
FIFTH CADET:          Why, it frightens ME
  To think of what will—
SIXTH CADET (*closing the door*): Something horrible
  Beyond imagination . . .
  (*They are all gone: some through the street door, some by the
  inner doors to right and left. A few disappear up the staircase.
  CYRANO and CHRISTIAN stand face to face a moment, and
  look at each other*)
CYRANO:                  To my arms!
CHRISTIAN:                          Sir? . . .
CYRANO: You have courage!
CHRISTIAN:              Oh, that! . . .
CYRANO:                          You are brave—
  That pleases me.

CHRISTIAN: You mean? . . .

CYRANO: Do you not know
I am her brother? Come!

CHRISTIAN: Whose?—

CYRANO: Hers—Roxane!

CHRISTIAN: Her . . . brother? You? (*Hurries to him*)

CYRANO: Her cousin. Much the same.

CHRISTIAN: And she has told you? . . .

CYRANO: Everything.

CHRISTIAN: She loves me?

CYRANO: Perhaps.

CHRISTIAN (*takes both his hands*):
My dear sir—more than I can say,
I am honoured—

CYRANO: This is rather sudden.

CHRISTIAN: Please
Forgive me—

CYRANO : Why, he is a handsome devil, This fellow!

CHRISTIAN: On my honour—if you knew
How much I have admired—

CYRANO: Yes, yes—and all
Those Noses which—

CHRISTIAN: Please! I apologize.

CYRANO (*change of tone*): Roxane expects a letter—

CHRISTIAN: Not from me?—

CYRANO: Yes. Why not?

CHRISTIAN: Once I write, that ruins all!

CYRANO: And why?

CHRISTIAN: Because . . . because I am a fool!
Stupid enough to hang myself!

CYRANO: But no—
You are no fool; you call yourself a fool,
There's proof enough in that. Besides, you did not
Attack me like a fool.

CHRISTIAN:                    Bah! Any one
     Can pick a quarrel. Yes, I have a sort
     Of rough-and-ready soldier's tongue. I know
     That. But with any woman—paralyzed,
     Speechless, dumb. I can only look at them.
     Yet sometimes, when I go away, their eyes . . .
CYRANO: Why not their hearts, if you should wait and see?
CHRISTIAN: No. I am one of those— I know—those men
     Who never can make love.
CYRANO:                         Strange. . . . Now it seems
     I, if I gave my mind to it, I might
     Perhaps make love well.
CHRISTIAN:                    Oh, if I had words
     To say what I have here!
CYRANO:                       If I could be
     A handsome little Musketeer with eyes!—
CHRISTIAN: Besides—you know Roxane—how sensitive—
     One rough word, and the sweet illusion—gone!
CYRANO: I wish you might be my interpreter.
CHRISTIAN: I wish I had your wit—
CYRANO:                          Borrow it, then!—
     Your beautiful young manhood—lend me that,
     And we two make one hero of romance!
CHRISTIAN: What?
CYRANO:          Would you dare repeat to her the words
     I gave you, day by day?
CHRISTIAN:                    You mean?
CYRANO:                                 I mean
     Roxane shall have no disillusionment!
     Come, shall we win her both together? Take
     The soul within this leathern jack of mine,
     And breathe it into you?       (*Touches him on the breast*)
                                So—there's my heart
     Under your velvet, now!
CHRISTIAN:                    But— Cyrano!—

CYRANO: But— Christian, why not?

CHRISTIAN: I am afraid—

CYRANO: I know—
Afraid that when you have her all alone,
You lose all. Have no fear. It is yourself
She loves—give her yourself put into words—
My words, upon your lips!

CHRISTIAN: But . . . but your eyes! . . .
They burn like—

CYRANO: Will you? . . . Will you?

CHRISTIAN: Does it mean so much to you?

CYRANO (*beside himself*): It means— (*recovers, changes tone*)
A Comedy,
A situation for a poet! Come,
Shall we collaborate? I'll be your cloak
Of darkness, your enchanted sword, your ring
To charm the fairy Princess!

CHRISTIAN: But the letter—
I cannot write—

CYRANO: Oh yes, the letter.
(*He takes from his pocket the letter which he has written*)
Here.

CHRISTIAN: What is this?

CYRANO: All there; all but the address.

CHRISTIAN: I—

CYRANO: Oh, you may send it. It will serve.

CHRISTIAN: But why
Have you done this?

CYRANO: I have amused myself
As we all do, we poets—writing vows
To Chloris, Phyllis—any pretty name—
You might have had a pocketful of them!
Take it, and turn to facts my fantasies—
I loosed these loves like doves into the air;
Give them a habitation and a home.

Here, take it— You will find me all the more
Eloquent, being insincere! Come!

CHRISTIAN:                              First,
There must be a few changes here and there—
Written at random, can it fit Roxane?

CYRANO: Like her own glove.

CHRISTIAN:                    No, but—

CYRANO:                          My son, have faith—
Faith in the love of women for themselves—
Roxane will know this letter for her own!

CHRISTIAN (*throws himself into the arms of* CYRANO. *They
embrace*): My friend!
(*The door upstage opens a little. A* CADET *steals in*)

THE CADET:        Nothing. A silence like the tomb . . .
I hardly dare look—                    (*he sees the two*)
                    Wha-at?
(*The other Cadets crowd in behind him and see*)

THE CADETS:              No!—No!

SECOND CADET:                    Mon dieu!

THE MUSKETEER (*slaps his knee*): Well, well, well!

CARBON:          Here's our devil . . . Christianized!
Offend one nostril, and he turns the other.

THE MUSKETEER:
Now we are allowed to talk about his nose!
(*Calls*) Hey, Lise! Come here—
                (*affectedly*) Snf! What a horrid smell!
What is it? . . .
(*Plants himself in front of* CYRANO, *and looks at his nose in
an impolite manner*)
                You ought to know about such things;
What seems to have died around here?

CYRANO (*knocks him backward over a bench*):  Cabbage-heads!
*Joy. The Cadets have found their old* CYRANO *again. General
disturbance.*
                    CURTAIN

# ACT III

## ROXANE'S KISS

*A little square in the old Marais: old houses, and a glimpse of narrow streets. On the right, THE HOUSE OF ROXANE and her garden wall, overhung with tall shrubbery. Over the door of the house a balcony and a tall window; to one side of the door, a bench. Ivy clings to the wall; jasmine embraces the balcony, trembles, and falls away.*

*By the bench and the jutting stonework of the wall one might easily climb up to the balcony.*

*Opposite, an ancient house of the like character, brick and stone, whose front door forms an entrance. The knocker on this door is tied up in linen like an injured thumb.*

*At the Curtain Rise* THE DUENNA *is seated on the bench beside the door. The window is wide open on* ROXANE'S *balcony; a light within suggests that it is early evening. By* THE DUENNA *stands* RAGUENEAU *dressed in what might be the livery of one attached to the household. He is by way of telling her something, and wiping his eyes meanwhile.*

RAGUENEAU:

    —And so she ran off with a Musketeer!
    I was ruined— I was alone— Remained
    Nothing for me to do but hang myself,
    So I did that. Presently along comes
    Monsieur de Bergerac, and cuts me down,
    And makes me steward to his cousin.

THE DUENNA:                           Ruined?—

    I thought your pastry was a great success!

RAGUENEAU (*shakes his head*):
> Lise loved the soldiers, and I loved the poets—
> Mars ate up all the cakes Apollo left;
> It did not take long. . . .

THE DUENNA (*calls up to window*):
>                              Roxane! Are you ready?
> We are late!

VOICE OF ROXANE (*within*): Putting on my cape—

THE DUENNA (*to* RAGUENEAU, *indicating the house opposite*):
>                              Clomire
> Across the way receives on Thursday nights—
> We are to have a psycho-colloquy
> Upon the Tender Passion.

RAGUENEAU:                    Ah—the Tender . . .

THE DUENNA (*sighs*): —Passion! . . .    (*Calls up to window*)
>              Roxane!—Hurry, dear—we shall miss
> The Tender Passion!

ROXANE:              Coming!—
> (*Music of stringed instruments off-stage approaching*)

THE VOICE OF CYRANO (*singing*):    La, la, la!—

THE DUENNA: A serenade?—How pleasant—

CYRANO:        •                    No, no, no!—
> F natural, you natural born fool!
> (*Enters, followed by two Pages, carrying large lutes*)

FIRST PAGE (*ironically*):
> No doubt your honour knows F natural
> When he hears—

CYRANO:              I am a musician, infant!—
> A pupil of Gassendi.

THE PAGE (*plays and sings*): La, la,—

CYRANO:                    Here—
> Give me that—
> (*he snatches the instrument from* THE PAGE *and continues the tune*)
>              La, la, la, la—

ROXANE (*appears on the balcony*):     Is that you,
     Cyrano?
CYRANO (*singing*): I, who praise your lilies fair,
     But long to love your ro . . . ses!
ROXANE:                              I'll be down—
     Wait—                         (*goes in through window*)
THE DUENNA: Did you train these virtuosi?
CYRANO:                              No—
     I won them on a bet from D'Assoucy.
     We were debating a fine point of grammar
     When, pointing out these two young nightingales
     Dressed up like peacocks, with their instruments,
     He cries: "No, but I KNOW! I'll wager you
     A day of music." Well, of course he lost;
     And so until to-morrow they are mine,
     My private orchestra. Pleasant at first,
     But they become a trifle—
     (*to the Pages*)                Here! Go play
     A minuet to Montfleury—and tell him
     I sent you!
     (*The Pages go up to the exit.* CYRANO *turns to* THE DUENNA)
                    I came here as usual
     To inquire after our friend—
     (*to Pages*)                Play out of tune.
     And keep on playing!
     (*The Pages go out. He turns to* THE DUENNA)
                    —Our friend with the great soul.
ROXANE (*enters in time to hear the last words*):
     He is beautiful and brilliant—and I love him!
CYRANO: Do you find Christian . . . intellectual?
ROXANE: More so than you, even.
CYRANO:                         I am glad.
ROXANE:                                   No man
     Ever so beautifully said those things—
     Those pretty nothings that are everything.

Sometimes he falls into a reverie;
His inspiration fails—then all at once,
He will say something absolutely . . . Oh! . . .

CYRANO: Really!

ROXANE:          How like a man! You think a man
Who has a handsome face must be a fool.

CYRANO:
He talks well about . . . matters of the heart?

ROXANE:
He does not *talk*; he rhapsodizes . . . dreams . . .

CYRANO (*twisting his moustache*): He . . . writes well?

ROXANE:                    Wonderfully. Listen now:
(*reciting as from memory*)
"Take my heart; I shall have it all the more;
Plucking the flowers, we keep the plant in bloom—"
Well?

CYRANO: Pooh!

ROXANE:          And this:
                         "Knowing you have in store
More heart to give than I to find heart-room—"

CYRANO:
First he has too much, then too little; just
How much heart does he need?

ROXANE (*tapping her foot*):          You are teasing me!
You are jealous!

CYRANO (*startled*):    Jealous?

ROXANE:                    Of his poetry—
You poets are like that . . .
                         And these last lines
Are they not the last word in tenderness?—
"There is no more to say: only believe
That unto you my whole heart gives one cry,
And writing, writes down more than you receive;
Sending you kisses through my finger-tips—
Lady, O read my letter with your lips!"

CYRANO: H'm, yes—those last lines . . . but he overwrites!

ROXANE: Listen to this—

CYRANO: You know them all by heart?

ROXANE: Every one!

CYRANO (*twisting his moustache*):

I may call that flattering . . .

ROXANE: He is a master!

CYRANO: Oh—come!

ROXANE: Yes—a master!

CYRANO (*bowing*): A master—if you will!

THE DUENNA (*comes downstage quickly*):

Monsieur de Guiche!—

(*To* CYRANO, *pushing him toward the house*)
Go inside— If he does not find you here,
It may be just as well. He may suspect—

ROXANE: —My secret! Yes; he is in love with me
And he is powerful. Let him not know—
One look would frost my roses before bloom.

CYRANO (*going into house*): Very well, very well!

ROXANE (*to* DE GUICHE, *as he enters*):

We were just going—

DE GUICHE: I came only to say farewell.

ROXANE: You leave
Paris?

DE GUICHE: Yes—for the front.

ROXANE: Ah!

DE GUICHE: And to-night!

ROXANE: Ah!

DE GUICHE: We have orders to besiege Arras.

ROXANE: Arras?

DE GUICHE: Yes. My departure leaves you . . . cold?

ROXANE (*politely*): Oh! Not that.

DE GUICHE: It has left me desolate—
When shall I see you? Ever? Did you know
I was made Colonel?

ROXANE (*indifferent*):        Bravo.
DE GUICHE:                Regiment
    Of the Guards.                •
ROXANE (*catching her breath*): Of the Guards?—
DE GUICHE:                        *His* regiment,
    Your cousin, the mighty man of words!—
    (*grimly*)                        Down there
    We may have an accounting!
ROXANE (*suffocating*):            Are you sure
    The Guards are ordered?
DE GUICHE:                Under my command!
ROXANE (*sinks down, breathless, on the bench; aside*):
    Christian!—
DE GUICHE:        What is it?
ROXANE (*losing control of herself*):        To the war—perhaps
    Never again to— When a woman cares,
    Is that nothing?
DE GUICHE (*surprised and delighted*):
                You say this now—to me—
    Now, at the very moment?—
ROXANE (*recovers—changes her tone*): Tell me something:
    My cousin— You say you mean to be revenged
    On him. Do you mean that?
DE GUICHE (*smiles*):            Why? Would you care?
ROXANE: Not for him.
DE GUICHE:            Do you see him?
ROXANE:                        Now and then.
DE GUICHE:
    He goes about everywhere nowadays
    With one of the Cadets—de Neuve—Neuville—
    Neuvillers—
ROXANE (*coolly*): A tall man?—
DE GUICHE:                Blond—
ROXANE:                        Rosy cheeks?—
DE GUICHE: Handsome!—

ROXANE:                          Pooh!—
DE GUICHE:                                And a fool.
ROXANE (*languidly*):              So he appears . . .
    (*animated*)
    But Cyrano? What will you do to him?
    Order him into danger? He loves that!
    I know what *I* should do.
DE GUICHE:                        What?
ROXANE:                                  Leave him here
    With his Cadets, while all the regiment
    Goes on to glory! That would torture him—
    To sit all through the war with folded arms—
    I know his nature. If you hate that man,
    Strike at his self-esteem.
DE GUICHE:                      Oh woman—woman!
    Who but a woman would have thought of this?
ROXANE:
    He'll eat his heart out, while his Gascon friends
    Bite their nails all day long in Paris here.
    And you will be avenged!
DE GUICHE:                    You love me then,
    A little? . . .
    (*she smiles*)
                    Making my enemies your own,
    Hating them—I should like to see in that
    A sign of love, Roxane.
ROXANE:                      Perhaps it is one . . .
DE GUICHE (*shows a number of folded despatches*):
    Here are the orders—for each company—
    Ready to send . . .
    (*selects one*) So— This is for the Guards—
    I'll keep that. Aha, Cyrano!
    (*To* ROXANE)           You too,
    You play your little games, do you?
ROXANE (*watching him*):                    Sometimes . . .

DE GUICHE (*close to her, speaking hurriedly*):
    And you!—Oh, I am mad over you!—
                                Listen—
    I leave to-night—but—let you through my hands
    Now, when I feel you trembling?—Listen— Close by,
    In the Rue d'Orléans, the Capuchins
    Have their new convent. By their law, no layman
    May pass inside those walls. I'll see to that—
    Their sleeves are wide enough to cover me—
    The servants of my Uncle-Cardinal
    Will fear his nephew. So—I'll come to you
    Masked, after everyone knows I have gone—
    Oh, let me wait one day!—
ROXANE:                If this be known,
    Your honour—
DE GUICHE:        Bah!
ROXANE:           The war—your duty—
DE GUICHE (*blows away an imaginary feather*):    Phoo!—
    Only say yes!
ROXANE:       No!
DE GUICHE:       Whisper . . .
ROXANE (*tenderly*):          I ought not
    To let you . . .
DE GUICHE:       Ah! . . .
ROXANE (*pretends to break down*): Ah, go!
    (*aside*)          —Christian remains—
    (*aloud—heroically*)
    I must have you a hero—Antoine . . .
DE GUICHE:                Heaven! . . .
    So you can love—
ROXANE:          One for whose sake I fear.
DE GUICHE (*triumphant*):          I go!
    Will that content you?          (*kisses her hand*)
ROXANE:         Yes—my friend!
    (*He goes out*)

THE DUENNA (*as* DE GUICHE *disappears, making a deep curtsey behind his back, and imitating* ROXANE'S *intense tone*): Yes—my friend!

ROXANE (*quickly, close to her*): Not a word to Cyrano—
He would never forgive me if he knew
I stole his war!

(*She calls toward the house*)
Cousin!
(CYRANO *comes out of the house; she turns to him, indicating the house opposite*) We are going over—
Alcandre speaks to-night—and Lysimon.

THE DUENNA (*puts finger in her ear*):
My little finger says we shall not hear
Everything.

CYRANO: Never mind me—

THE DUENNA (*across the street*): Look— Oh, look!
The knocker tied up in a napkin— Yes,
They muzzled you because you bark too loud
And interrupt the lecture—little beast!

ROXANE (*as the door opens*): Enter . . .
(*to* CYRANO) If Christian comes, tell him to wait.

CYRANO: Oh—

(ROXANE *returns*)
When he comes, what will you talk about?
You always know beforehand.

ROXANE: About . . .

CYRANO: Well?

ROXANE: You will not tell him, will you?

CYRANO: I am dumb.

ROXANE:
About nothing! Or about everything—
I shall say: "Speak of love in your own words—
Improvise! Rhapsodize! Be eloquent!"

CYRANO (*smiling*): Good!

ROXANE: Sh!—

CYRANO:                Sh!—

ROXANE:               Not a word!
     (*She goes in; the door closes*)

CYRANO (*bowing*):             Thank you so much—

ROXANE (*opens door and puts out her head*):
     He must be unprepared—

CYRANO:            Of course!

ROXANE:                Sh!—
     (*goes in again*)

CYRANO (*calls*):                Christian!
     (CHRISTIAN *enters*)
     I have your theme—bring on your memory!—
     Here is your chance now to surpass yourself,
     No time to lose— Come! Look intelligent—
     Come home and learn your lines.

CHRISTIAN:           No.

CYRANO:            What?

CHRISTIAN:             I'll wait
     Here for Roxane.

CYRANO:       What lunacy is this?
     Come quickly!

CHRISTIAN:      No, I say! I have had enough—
     Taking my words, my letters, all from you—
     Making our love a little comedy!
     It was a game at first; but now—she cares . . .
     Thanks to you. I am not afraid. I'll speak
     For myself now.

CYRANO:       Undoubtedly!

CHRISTIAN:             I will!
     Why not? I am no such fool—you shall see!
     Besides—my dear friend—you have taught me much:
     I ought to know something . . . By God, I know
     Enough to take a woman in my arms!
     (ROXANE *appears in the doorway, opposite*)
     There she is now . . . Cyrano, wait! Stay here!

CYRANO (*bows*): Speak for yourself, my friend!

                               (*He goes out*)

ROXANE (*taking leave of the company*):       —Barthénoide!
   Alcandre! . . . Grémione! . . .

THE DUENNA:               I told you so—
   We missed the Tender Passion!
   (*She goes into* ROXANE's *house*)

ROXANE:                 Urimédonte!—
   Adieu!
   (*As the guests disappear down the street, she turns to*
   CHRISTIAN)
         Is that you, Christian? Let us stay
   Here, in the twilight. They are gone. The air
   Is fragrant. We shall be alone. Sit down
   There—so . . .            (*they sit on the bench*)
         Now tell me things.

CHRISTIAN (*after a silence*):      I love you.

ROXANE (*closes her eyes*):              Yes,
   Speak to me about love . . .

CHRISTIAN:           I love you.

ROXANE:                 Now
   Be eloquent! . . .

CHRISTIAN:        I love—

ROXANE (*opens her eyes*):     You have your theme—
   Improvise! Rhapsodize!

CHRISTIAN:        I love you so!

ROXANE: Of course. And then? . . .

CHRISTIAN:         And then . . . Oh, I should be
   So happy if you loved me too! Roxane,
   Say that you love me too!

ROXANE (*making a face*):    I ask for cream—
   You give me milk and water. Tell me first
   A little, how you love me.

CHRISTIAN:         Very much.

ROXANE: Oh—tell me how you *feel*!

CHRISTIAN (*coming nearer, and devouring her with his eyes*):

           Your throat . . . If only
  I might . . . kiss it—

ROXANE:      Christian!

CHRISTIAN:        I love you so!

ROXANE (*makes as if to rise*): Again?

CHRISTIAN (*desperately, restraining her*):

      No, not again— I do not love you—

ROXANE (*settles back*): That is better . . .

CHRISTIAN:      I adore you!

ROXANE:          Oh!—
  (*rises and moves away*)

CHRISTIAN:          I know;
  I grow absurd.

ROXANE (*coldly*):  And that displeases me
  As much as if you had grown ugly.

CHRISTIAN:        I—

ROXANE: Gather your dreams together into words!

CHRISTIAN: I love—

ROXANE:    I know; you love me. Adieu.
  (*She goes to the house*)

CHRISTIAN:         No,
  But wait—please—let me— I was going to say—

ROXANE (*pushes the door open*):
  That you adore me. Yes; I know that too.
  No! . . . Go away! . . .
  (*She goes in and shuts the door in his face*)

CHRISTIAN:     I . . . I . . .

CYRANO (*enters*):      A great success!

CHRISTIAN: Help me!

CYRANO:    Not I.

CHRISTIAN:      I cannot live unless
  She loves me—now, this moment!

CYRANO:         How the devil
  Am I to teach you now—this moment?

CHRISTIAN (*catches him by the arm*):          —Wait!—
     Look! Up there!—Quick—
     (*The light shows in* ROXANE'S *window*)
CYRANO:                    Her window—
CHRISTIAN (*wailing*):                    I shall die!—
CYRANO: Less noise!
CHRISTIAN:          Oh, I—
CYRANO:               It does seem fairly dark—
CHRISTIAN (*excitedly*): Well?—Well?—Well?—
CYRANO:                    Let us try what can be done;
     It is more than you deserve—stand over there,
     Idiot—there!—before the balcony—
     Let me stand underneath. I'll whisper you
     What to say.
CHRISTIAN:          She may hear—she may—
CYRANO:                         Less noise!
     (*The Pages appear upstage*)
FIRST PAGE: Hep!—
CYRANO (*finger to lips*): Sh!—
FIRST PAGE (*low voice*):          We serenaded Montfleury!—
     What next?
CYRANO:          Down to the corner of the street—
     One this way—and the other over there—
     If anybody passes, play a tune!
PAGE: What tune, O musical Philosopher?
CYRANO: Sad for a man, or merry for a woman—
     Now go!
     (*The Pages disappear, one toward each corner of the street*)
CYRANO (*to* CHRISTIAN): Call her!
CHRISTIAN:          Roxane!
CYRANO:                    Wait . . .
     (*gathers up a handful of pebbles*)     Gravel . . .
     (*throws it at the window*)                    There!—
ROXANE (*opens the window*): Who is calling?
CHRISTIAN:                    I—
     4

ROXANE:                                        Who?
CHRISTIAN:                                     Christian.
ROXANE: You again?
CHRISTIAN:          I had to tell you—
CYRANO (*under the balcony*):
                              Good— Keep your voice down.
ROXANE: No. Go away. You tell me nothing.
CHRISTIAN:                              Please!—
ROXANE: You do not love me any more—
CHRISTIAN (*to whom* CYRANO *whispers his words*):
                                        No—no—
    Not any more— I love you . . . evermore . . .
    And ever . . . more and more!
ROXANE (*about to close the window—pauses*):
                                        A little better . . .
CHRISTIAN (*same business*):
    Love grows and struggles like . . . an angry child . . .
    Breaking my heart . . . his cradle . . .
ROXANE (*coming out on the balcony*):          Better still—
    But . . . such a babe is dangerous; why not
    Have smothered it new-born?
CHRISTIAN:                        And so I do . . .
    And yet he lives . . . I found . . . as you shall
        find . . .
    This new-born babe . . . an infant . . . Hercules!
ROXANE (*further forward*): Good!—
CHRISTIAN:
        Strong enough . . . at birth . . . to strangle those
    Two serpents—Doubt and . . . Pride.
ROXANE (*leans over balcony*):              Why, very well!
    Tell me now why you speak so haltingly—
    Has your imagination gone lame?
CYRANO (*thrusts* CHRISTIAN *under the balcony, and stands in his
    place*):                              Here—
    This grows too difficult

ROXANE:               Your words to-night
    Hesitate. Why?
CYRANO (*in a low tone, imitating* CHRISTIAN):
              Through the warm summer gloom
    They grope in darkness toward the light of you.
ROXANE: My words, well aimed, find you more readily.
CYRANO:
    My heart is open wide and waits for them—
    Too large a mark to miss! My words fly home,
    Heavy with honey like returning bees,
    To your small secret ear. Moreover—yours
    Fall to me swiftly. Mine more slowly rise.
ROXANE: Yet not so slowly as they did at first.
CYRANO:
    They have learned the way, and you have welcomed
       them.
ROXANE (*softly*): Am I so far above you now?
CYRANO:                     So far—
    If you let fall upon me one hard word,
    Out of that height—you crush me!
ROXANE (*turns*):             I'll come down—
CYRANO (*quickly*): No!
ROXANE (*points out the bench under the balcony*):
              Stand you on the bench. Come nearer!
CYRANO (*recoils into the shadow*): No!—
ROXANE:           And why—so great a *No*?
CYRANO (*more and more overcome by emotion*):   Let me enjoy
    The one moment I ever—my one chance
    To speak to you . . . unseen!
ROXANE:            Unseen?—
CYRANO:              Yes!—yes . . .
    Night, making all things dimly beautiful,
    One veil over us both— You only see
    The darkness of a long cloak in the gloom,
    And I the whiteness of a summer gown—

You are all light— I am all shadow! . . . How.
Can you know what this moment means to me?
If I was ever eloquent—

ROXANE: You were
Eloquent—

CYRANO: —You have never heard till now
My own heart speaking!

ROXANE: Why not?

CYRANO: Until now,
I spoke through . . .

ROXANE: Yes?—

CYRANO: —through that sweet drunkenness
You pour into the world out of your eyes!
But to-night . . . but to-night, I indeed speak
For the first time!

ROXANE: For the first time— Your voice,
Even, is not the same.

CYRANO (*passionately; moves nearer*):
How should it be?
I have another voice to-night—my own,
Myself, daring—
(*he stops, confused; then tries to recover himself*)
Where was I? . . . I forget! . . .
Forgive me. This is all sweet like a dream . . .
Strange—like a dream . . .

ROXANE: How, strange?

CYRANO: Is it not so
To be myself to you, and have no fear
Of moving you to laughter?

ROXANE: Laughter—why?

CYRANO (*struggling for an explanation*):
Because . . . What am I . . . What is any man,
That he dare ask for you? Therefore my heart
Hides behind phrases. There's a modesty
In these things too— I come here to pluck down

Out of the sky the evening star—then smile,
And stoop to gather little flowers.

ROXANE:                   Are they
Not sweet, those little flowers?

CYRANO:               Not enough sweet
For you and me, to-night!

ROXANE (*breathless*):        You never spoke
To me like this . . .

CYRANO:             Little things, pretty things—
Arrows and hearts and torches—roses red,
And violets blue—are these all? Come away,
And breathe fresh air! Must we keep on and on
Sipping stale honey out of tiny cups
Decorated with golden tracery,
Drop by drop, all day long? We are alive;
We thirst— Come away, plunge, and drink, and drown
In the great river flowing to the sea!

ROXANE: But . . . Poetry?

CYRANO:             I have made rhymes for you—
Not now— Shall we insult Nature, this night,
These flowers, this moment—shall we set all these
To phrases from a letter by Voiture?
Look once at the high stars that shine in heaven,
And put off artificiality!
Have you not seen great gaudy hothouse flowers,
Barren, without fragrance?—Souls are like that:
Forced to show all, they soon become all show—
The means to Nature's end ends meaningless!

ROXANE: But . . . Poetry?

CYRANO:          Love hates that game of words!
It is a crime to fence with life— I tell you,
There comes one moment, once—and God help those
Who pass that moment by!—when Beauty stands
Looking into the soul with grave, sweet eyes
That sicken at pretty words!

ROXANE:                              If that be true—
    And when that moment comes to you and me—
    What words will you? . . .
CYRANO:                          All those, all those, all those
    That blossom in my heart, I'll fling to you—
    Armfuls of loose bloom! Love, I love beyond
    Breath, beyond reason, beyond love's own power
    Of loving! Your name is like a golden bell
    Hung in my heart; and when I think of you,
    I tremble, and the bell swings and rings—
                                    "Roxane!" . . .
    "Roxane!" . . . along my veins, "Roxane!" . . .
                                        I know
    All small forgotten things that once meant You—
    I remember last year, the First of May,
    A little before noon, you had your hair
    Drawn low, that one time only. Is that strange?
    You know how, after looking at the sun,
    One sees red suns everywhere—so, for hours
    After the flood of sunshine that you are,
    My eyes are blinded by your burning hair!
ROXANE (*very low*): Yes . . . that is . . . Love—
CYRANO:                          Yes, that is Love—that wind
    Of terrible and jealous beauty, blowing
    Over me—that dark fire, that music . . .
                                        Yet
    Love seeketh not his own! Dear, you may take
    My happiness to make you happier,
    Even though you never know I gave it you—
    Only let me hear sometimes, all alone,
    The distant laughter of your joy! . . .
                                        I never
    Look at you, but there's some new virtue born
    In me, some new courage. Do you begin
    To understand, a little? Can you feel

My soul, there in the darkness, breathe on you?
—Oh, but to-night, now, I dare say these things—
I . . . to you . . . and you hear them! . . . It is too
    much!
In my most sweet unreasonable dreams,
I have not hoped for this! Now let me die,
Having lived. It is my voice, mine, my own,
That makes you tremble there in the green gloom
Above me—for you do tremble, as a blossom
Among the leaves— You tremble, and I can feel,
All the way down along these jasmine branches,
Whether you will or no, the passion of you
Trembling . . .
(*he kisses wildly the end of a drooping spray of jasmine*)

ROXANE:        Yes, I do tremble . . . and I weep . . .
And I love you . . . and I am yours . . . and you
Have made me thus!

CYRANO (*after a pause; quietly*):
                What is death like, I wonder?
I know everything else now . . .
                        I have done
This, to you—I, myself . . .
                  Only let me
Ask one thing more—

CHRISTIAN (*under the balcony*):
              One kiss!

ROXANE (*startled*):        One?—

CYRANO (*to* CHRISTIAN):        You! . . .

ROXANE:                You ask me
For—

CYRANO: I . . . Yes, but—I mean—
    (*to* CHRISTIAN)        You go too far!

CHRISTIAN: She is willing!—Why not make the most of it?

CYRANO (*to* ROXANE):
I did ask . . . but I know I ask too much . . .

ROXANE: Only one— Is that all?

CYRANO:                          All!—How much more
Than all!—I know—I frighten you—I ask . . .
I ask you to refuse—

CHRISTIAN (*to* CYRANO):  But why? Why? Why?

CYRANO: Christian, be quiet!

ROXANE (*leaning over*):          What is that you say
To yourself?

CYRANO:          I am angry with myself
Because I go too far, and so I say
To myself: "Christian, be quiet!"—
(*The lutes begin to play*)          Hark—someone
Is coming—
(ROXANE *closes her window.* CYRANO *listens to the lutes,
one of which plays a gay melody, the other a mournful one*)
          A sad tune, a merry tune—
Man, woman—what do they mean?—
(*A* CAPUCHIN *enters; he carries a lantern, and goes from
house to house, looking at the doors*)
                              Aha!—a priest!

(*To* THE CAPUCHIN)
What is this new game of Diogenes?

THE CAPUCHIN: I am looking for the house of Madame—

CHRISTIAN (*impatient*):                          Bah!—

THE CAPUCHIN: Madeleine Robin—

CHRISTIAN:                    What does he want?

CYRANO (*to* THE CAPUCHIN; *points out a street*):  This way—
To the right—keep to the right—

THE CAPUCHIN:                    I thank you, sir!—
I'll say my beads for you to the last grain.

CYRANO: Good fortune, father, and my service to you!
(THE CAPUCHIN *goes out*)

CHRISTIAN: Win me that kiss!

CYRANO:              No.

CHRISTIAN:                    Sooner or later—

CYRANO:                                                    True . . .
    That is true . . . Soon or late, it will be so
  . Because you are young and she is beautiful—
    (*To himself*) Since it must be, I had rather be myself
    (*The window re-opens.* CHRISTIAN *hides under the balcony*)
    The cause of . . . what must be.
ROXANE (*out on the balcony*):              Are you still there?
    We were speaking of—
CYRANO:                    A kiss. The word is sweet—
    What will the deed be? Are your lips afraid
    Even of its burning name? Not much afraid—
    Not too much! Have you not unwittingly
    Laid aside laughter, slipping beyond speech
    Insensibly, already, without fear,
    From words to smiles . . . from smiles to sighs . . .
        from sighing,   .
    Even to tears? One step more—only one—
    From a tear to a kiss—one step, one thrill!
ROXANE: Hush!—
CYRANO:        And what is a kiss, when all is done?
    A promise given under seal—a vow
    Taken before the shrine of memory—
    A signature acknowledged—a rosy dot
    Over the i of Loving—a secret whispered
    To listening lips apart—a moment made
    Immortal, with a rush of wings unseen—
    A sacrament of blossoms, a new song
    Sung by two hearts to an old simple tune—
    The ring of one horizon around two souls
    Together, all alone!
ROXANE:                Hush! . . .
.CYRANO:                        Why, what shame?—
    There was a Queen of France, not long ago
    And a great lord of England—a queen's gift,
    A crown jewel!—
        4*

ROXANE:                    Indeed!
CYRANO:                         Indeed, like him,
   I have my sorrows and my silences;
   Like her, you are the queen I dare adore;
   Like him I am faithful and forlorn—
ROXANE:                              Like him,
   Beautiful—
CYRANO (*aside*): So I am—I forgot that!
ROXANE:
   Then— Come! . . . Gather your sacred blossom . . .
CYRANO (*to* CHRISTIAN): Go!—
ROXANE:                    Your crown jewel . . .
CYRANO:                              Go on!—
ROXANE: Your old new song . . .
CYRANO:                    Climb!—
CHRISTIAN (*hesitates*):    No— Would you?—not yet—
ROXANE:                         Your moment made
   Immortal . . .
CYRANO (*pushing him*): Climb up, animal!
   (CHRISTIAN *springs on the bench, and climbs by the pillars,*
   *the branches, the vines, until he bestrides the balcony railing*)
CHRISTIAN:                    Roxane! . . .
   (*he takes her in his arms and bends over her*)
CYRANO (*very low*): Ah! . . . Roxane! . . .
                    I have won what I have won—
   The feast of love—and I am Lazarus!
   Yet . . . I have something here that is mine now
   And was not mine before I spoke the words
   That won her—not for me! . . . Kissing my words
   My words, upon your lips!
   (*The lutes begin to play*)
                    A merry tune—
   A sad tune— So! The Capuchin!
   (*He pretends to be running, as if he had arrived from a distance;*
   *then calls up to the balcony*)          Hola!

ROXANE: Who is it?

CYRANO:                    I. Is Christian there with you?

CHRISTIAN (*astonished*): Cyrano!

ROXANE:                    Good morrow, Cousin!

CYRANO:                    Cousin, . . . good morrow!

ROXANE: I am coming down.

> (*She disappears into the house.* THE CAPUCHIN *enters up-
> stage*)

CHRISTIAN (*sees him*):        Oh—again!

THE CAPUCHIN (*to* CYRANO):        She lives *here*,
    Madeleine Robin!

CYRANO:        You said RO-LIN.

THE CAPUCHIN:                No—
    R-O-B-I-N

ROXANE (*appears on the threshold of the house, followed by*
    RAGUENEAU *with a lantern, and by* CHRISTIAN):
                What is it?

THE CAPUCHIN:        A letter.

CHRISTIAN:                Oh! . . .

THE CAPUCHIN (*to* ROXANE):
    Some matter profitable to the soul—
    A very noble lord gave it to me!

ROXANE (*to* CHRISTIAN): De Guiche!

CHRISTIAN:                He dares?—

ROXANE:                It will not be for long;
    When he learns that I love you . . .
    (*By the light of the lantern which* RAGUENEAU *holds, she
    reads the letter in a low tone, as if to herself*)
                        "Mademoiselle
    The drums are beating, and the regiment
    Arms for the march. Secretly I remain
    Here, in the Convent. I have disobeyed;
    I shall be with you soon. I send this first
    By an old monk, as simple as a sheep,
    Who understands nothing of this. Your smile

Is more than I can bear, and seek no more.
Be alone to-night, waiting for one who dares
To hope you will forgive . . . —" etcetera—
(*to* THE CAPUCHIN)
Father, this letter concerns you . . .
(*to* CHRISTIAN)                               —and you.
Listen:
(*The others gather around her. She pretends to read from the letter, aloud*)
          "Mademoiselle:
                              The Cardinal
Will have his way, although against your will;
That is why I am sending this to you
By a most holy man, intelligent,
Discreet. You will communicate to him
Our order to perform, here and at once
The rite of . . .
(*turns the page*)
                              —Holy Matrimony. You
And Christian will be married privately
In your house. I have sent him to you. I know
You hesitate. Be resigned, nevertheless,
To the Cardinal's command, who sends herewith
His blessing. Be assured also of my own
Respect and high consideration—*signed*,
Your very humble and—etcetera—"
THE CAPUCHIN:
    A noble lord! I said so—never fear—
    A worthy lord!—a very worthy lord!—
ROXANE (*to* CHRISTIAN): Am I a good reader of letters?
CHRISTIAN (*motions toward* THE CAPUCHIN):          Careful!—
ROXANE (*in a tragic tone*): Oh, this is terrible!
THE CAPUCHIN (*turns the light of his lantern on* CYRANO):
                                                    You are to be—

CHRISTIAN: *I* am the bridegroom!

THE CAPUCHIN (*turns his lantern upon* CHRISTIAN; *then, as if some suspicion crossed his mind, upon seeing the young man so handsome*):          Oh—why, *you* . . .

ROXANE (*quickly*):                Look here—
"Postscript: Give to the Convent in my name
One hundred and twenty pistoles"—

THE CAPUCHIN:              Think of it!
A worthy lord—a very worthy lord! . . .
(*To* ROXANE, *solemnly*)
Daughter, resign yourself!

ROXANE (*with an air of martyrdom*): I am resigned . . .
(*While* RAGUENEAU *opens the door for* THE CAPUCHIN *and*
CHRISTIAN *invites him to enter, she turns to* CYRANO)
De Guiche may come. Keep him out here with you
Do not let him—

CYRANO:         I understand!
(*To* THE CAPUCHIN)         How long will you be?—

THE CAPUCHIN:    Oh, a quarter of an hour.

CYRANO (*hurrying them into the house*):
Hurry—I'll wait here—

ROXANE (*to* CHRISTIAN):    Come!    (*They go into the house*)

CYRANO:                Now then, to make
His Grace delay that quarter of an hour . . .
I have it!—up here—
(*He steps on the bench, and climbs up the wall toward the balcony. The lutes begin to play a mournful melody*)
            Sad music— Ah, a man! . . .
(*The music pauses on a sinister tremolo*)
Oh—very much a man!
(*He sits astride of the railing and, drawing toward him a long branch of one of the trees which border the garden wall, he grasps it with both hands, ready to swing himself down*)
            So—not too high—
(*He peers down at the ground*)
I must float gently through the atmosphere—

DE GUICHE (*enters, masked, groping in the dark toward the house*):
  Where is that cursed, bleating Capuchin?
CYRANO:
  What if he knows my voice?—the devil!—Tic-tac,
  Bergerac—we unlock our Gascon tongue;
  A good strong accent—
DE GUICHE:                    Here is the house—all dark—
  Damn this mask!—
  (*As he is about to enter the house,* CYRANO *leaps from the
  balcony, still holding fast to the branch, which bends and
  swings him between* DE GUICHE *and the door; then he
  releases the branch and pretends to fall heavily as though from
  a height. He lands flatly on the ground, where he lies motionless,
  as if stunned.* DE GUICHE *leaps back*)
                    What is that?
  (*When he lifts his eyes, the branch has sprung back into place.
  He can see nothing but the sky; he does not understand*)
                    Why . . . where did this man
  Fall from?
CYRANO (*sits up, and speaks with a strong accent*):
          —The moon!
DE GUICHE:          You—
CYRANO:                    From the moon, the moon!
  I fell out of the moon!
DE GUICHE:              The fellow is mad—
CYRANO (*dreamily*): Where am I?
DE GUICHE:              Why—
CYRANO:                    What time is it? What place
  Is this? What day? What season?
DE GUICHE:                    You—
CYRANO:                              I am stunned!
DE GUICHE: My dear sir—
CYRANO:              Like a bomb—a bomb—I fell
  From the moon!
DE GUICHE:        Now, see here—

CYRANO (*rising to his feet, and speaking in a terrible voice*):
                    I say, the moon!
DE GUICHE (*recoils*): Very well—if you say so—
    (*aside*)                              Raving mad!—
CYRANO (*advancing upon him*):
    I am not speaking metaphorically!
DE GUICHE: Pardon.
CYRANO:           A hundred years—an hour ago—
    I really cannot say how long I fell—
    I was in yonder shining sphere—
DE GUICHE (*shrugs his shoulders*):        Quite so.
    Please let me pass.
CYRANO (*interposes himself*):
                    Where am I? Tell the truth—
    I can bear it. In what quarter of the globe
    Have I descended like a meteorite?
DE GUICHE: Morbleu!
CYRANO:             I could not choose my place to fall—
    The earth spun round so fast— Was it the Earth,
    I wonder?—Or is this another world?
    Another moon? Whither have I been drawn
    By the dead weight of my posterior?
CYRANO (*with a sudden cry, which causes* DE GUICHE *to recoil
    again*): His face! My God—black!
DE GUICHE (*carries his hand to his mask*):        Oh!—
CYRANO (*terrified*): Are you a native? Is this Africa?
DE GUICHE: —This mask!
CYRANO (*somewhat reassured*): Are we in Venice? Genoa?
DE GUICHE (*tries to pass him*): A lady is waiting for me.
CYRANO (*quite happy again*):                So this is Paris!
DE GUICHE (*smiling in spite of himself*):
    This fool becomes amusing.
CYRANO:                    Ah! You smile?
DE GUICHE: I do. Kindly permit me—

CYRANO (*delighted*):                    Dear old Paris—
    Well, well!—
    (*wholly at his ease, smiles, bows, arranges his dress*)
                    Excuse my appearance. I arrive
    By the last thunderbolt—a trifle singed
    As I came through the ether. These long journeys—
    You know! There are so few conveniences!
    My eyes are full of star-dust. On my spurs,
    Some sort of fur . . . Planet's apparently . . .
    (*Plucks something from his sleeve*)
    Look—on my doublet— That's a Comet's hair!
    (*He blows something from the back of his hand*)
    Phoo!

DE GUICHE (*grows angry*): Monsieur—

CYRANO (*as* DE GUICHE *is about to push past, thrusts his leg in
    the way*):                    Here's a tooth, stuck in my boot,
    From the Great Bear. Trying to get away,
    I tripped over the Scorpion and came down
    Slap, into one scale of the Balances—
    The pointer marks my weight this moment . . .
    (*Pointing upward*)                             See?
    (DE GUICHE *makes a sudden movement.* CYRANO *catches
    his arm*)
    Be careful! If you struck me on the nose,
    It would drip milk!

DE GUICHE:              Milk?

CYRANO:                    From the Milky Way!

DE GUICHE: Hell!

CYRANO:          No, no—Heaven.
    (*Crossing his arms*)                    Curious place up there—
    Did you know Sirius wore a nightcap? True!
    (*Confidentially*)
    The Little Bear is still too young to bite.
    (*Laughing*)
    My foot caught in the Lyre, and broke a string.

*(Proudly)*

Well—when I write my book, and tell the tale
Of my adventures—all these little stars
That shake out of my cloak—I must save those
To use for asterisks!

DE GUICHE:                That will do now—
I wish—

CYRANO:     Yes, yes—I know—

DE GUICHE:                         Sir—

CYRANO:                                   You desire
To learn from my own lips the character
Of the moon's surface—its inhabitants.   If any—

DE GUICHE *(loses patience and shouts)*:
I desire no such thing! I—

CYRANO *(rapidly)*:
You wish to know by what mysterious means
I reached the moon?—well—confidentially—
It was a new invention of my own.

DE GUICHE *(discouraged)*: Drunk too—as well as mad!

CYRANO:                                   I scorned the eagle
Of Regiomontanus, and the dove
Of Archytas!

DE GUICHE:     A learned lunatic!—

CYRANO:
I imitated no one. I myself
Discovered not one scheme merely, but six—
Six ways to violate the virgin sky!

*(DE GUICHE has succeeded in passing him, and moves toward
the door of ROXANE's house. CYRANO follows, ready to use
violence if necessary)*

DE GUICHE *(looks around)*: Six?

CYRANO *(with increasing volubility)*:
                    As for instance—Having stripped myself
Bare as a wax candle, adorn my form
With crystal vials filled with morning dew,

And so be drawn aloft, as the sun rises
Drinking the mist of dawn!

DE GUICHE (*takes a step toward* CYRANO):

Yes—that makes one.

CYRANO (*draws back to lead him away from the door; speaks faster and faster*):

Or, sealing up the air in a cedar chest,
Rarefy it by means of mirrors, placed
In an icosahedron.

DE GUICHE (*takes another step*): Two.

CYRANO (*still retreating*):                    Again,
I might construct a rocket, in the form
Of a huge locust, driven by impulses
Of villainous saltpetre from the rear,
Upward, by leaps and bounds.

DE GUICHE (*interested in spite of himself, and counting on his fingers*):                    Three.

CYRANO:                                Or again,
Smoke having a natural tendency to rise,
Blow in a globe enough to raise me.

DE GUICHE (*more and more astonished*):    Four!

CYRANO:
Or since Diana, as old fables tell,
Draws forth to fill her crescent horn, the marrow
Of bulls and goats—to annoint myself therewith.

DE GUICHE (*hypnotized*): Five!—

CYRANO (*has by this time led him all the way across the street, close to a bench*):    Finally—seated on an iron plate,
To hurl a magnet in the air—the iron
Follows—I catch the magnet—throw again—
And so proceed indefinitely.

DE GUICHE:                    Six!—
All excellent,—and which did you adopt?

CYRANO (*coolly*): Why, none of them. . . . A seventh.

DE GUICHE:                                Which was?—

CYRANO: Guess!—

DE GUICHE: An interesting idiot, this!

CYRANO (*imitates the sound of waves with his voice, and their movement by large, vague gestures*):

Hoo! . . . Hoo! . . .

DE GUICHE: Well?

CYRANO: Have you guessed it yet?

DE GUICHE: Why, no.

CYRANO (*grandiloquent*): The ocean! . . .
What hour its rising tide seeks the full moon,
I laid me on the strand, fresh from the spray,
My head fronting the moonbeams, since the hair
Retains moisture—and so I slowly rose
As upon angels' wings, effortlessly,
Upward—then suddenly I felt a shock!—
And then . . .

DE GUICHE (*overcome by curiosity, sits down on the bench*):
And then?

CYRANO: And then—
(*changes abruptly to his natural voice*)
The time is up!—
Fifteen minutes, your Grace!—You are now free;
And—they are bound—in wedlock.

DE GUICHE (*leaping up*): Am *I* drunk?
That voice . . .
(*The door of* ROXANE's *house opens; lackeys appear, bearing lighted candles. Lights up.* CYRANO *removes his hat*)
And that nose!—Cyrano!

CYRANO (*saluting*): Cyrano! . . .
This very moment, they have exchanged rings.

DE GUICHE: Who?
(*He turns upstage. Between the lackeys,* ROXANE *and* CHRISTIAN *appear, hand in hand.* THE CAPUCHIN *follows them, smiling.* RAGUENEAU *holds aloft a torch.* THE

DUENNA *brings up the rear, in a negligée, and a pleasant flutter of emotion*)

                              Zounds!

(*To* ROXANE)            You?—

(*Recognizes* CHRISTIAN)            He?—

(*Saluting* ROXANE)            My sincere compliments!

(*To* CYRANO)

You also, my inventor of machines!
Your rigmarole would have detained a saint
Entering Paradise—decidedly
You must not fail to write that book some day!

CYRANO (*bowing*): Sir, I engage myself to do so.
    (*Leads the bridal pair down to* DE GUICHE *and strokes with great satisfaction his long white beard*)

THE CAPUCHIN:                              My lord,
    The handsome couple you—and God—have joined
    Together!

DE GUICHE (*regarding him with a frosty eye*): Quite so.
    (*Turns to* ROXANE)            Madame, kindly bid
    Your . . . husband farewell.

ROXANE:                              Oh!—

DE GUICHE (*to* CHRISTIAN):            Your regiment
    Leaves to-night, sir. Report at once!

ROXANE:                              You mean
    For the front? The war?

DE GUICHE:            Certainly!

ROXANE:                              I thought
    The Cadets were not going—

DE GUICHE:            Oh yes, they are!
    (*Taking out the despatch from his pocket*)
    Here is the order—
    (*to* CHRISTIAN)            Baron! Deliver this.

ROXANE (*throws herself into* CHRISTIAN'S *arms*):            CHRISTIAN!

DE GUICHE (*to* CYRANO, *sneering*):
                              The bridal night is not so near!

CYRANO (*aside*): Somehow that news fails to disquiet me.

CHRISTIAN (*to* ROXANE): Your lips again . . .

CYRANO:                There . . . That will do now— Come!

CHRISTIAN (*still holding* ROXANE):

    You do not know how hard it is—

CYRANO (*tries to drag him away*):        I know!
    (*The beating of drums is heard in the distance*)

DE GUICHE: The regiment—on the march!

ROXANE (*as* CYRANO *tries to lead* CHRISTIAN *away, follows,
    and detains them*):                Take care of him
    For me—
    (*appealingly*) Promise me never to let him do
    Anything dangerous!

CYRANO:                I'll do my best—
    I cannot promise—

ROXANE:        Make him be careful!

CYRANO:                        Yes—
    I'll try—

ROXANE:    Be sure you keep him dry and warm!

CYRANO: Yes, yes—if possible—

ROXANE (*confidentially, in his ear*): See that he remains
    Faithful!—

CYRANO:        Of course! If—

ROXANE:                And have him write to me
    Every single day!

CYRANO (*stops*):    That, I promise you!

CURTAIN

# ACT IV

## THE CADETS OF GASCOYNE

THE POST *occupied by the Company of* CARBON DE CASTEL-JALOUX *at* THE SIEGE OF ARRAS.
*In the background, a rampart traversing the entire scene; beyond this, and apparently below, a plain stretches away to the horizon. The country is cut up with earthworks and other suggestions of the siege. In the distance, against the sky-line, the houses and the walls of Arras.*
*Tents; scattered weapons; drums, et cetera. It is near daybreak, and the east is yellow with approaching dawn. Sentries at intervals. Camp-fires.*
*Curtain Rise discovers the Cadets asleep, rolled in their cloaks.*
CARBON DE CASTEL-JALOUX *and* LE BRET *keep watch. They are both very thin and pale.* CHRISTIAN *is asleep among the others, wrapped in his cloak, in the foreground, his face lighted by the flickering fire. Silence.*

LE BRET: Horrible!

CARBON: Why, yes. All of that.

LE BRET: Mordious!

CARBON (*gesture toward the sleeping Cadets*):
    Swear gently— You might wake them.
    (*To Cadets*) Go to sleep—Hush!
    (*To* LE BRET) Who sleeps dines.

LE BRET: I have insomnia.
    God! What a famine.
    (*Firing off-stage*)

CARBON: Curse that musketry!
    They'll wake my babies.
    (*To the men*)               Go to sleep!—
A CADET (*rouses*):               Diantre!   Again?
CARBON:   No—only Cyrano coming home.
    (*The heads which have been raised sink back again*)
A SENTRY (*off-stage*): Halt! Who goes there?
VOICE OF CYRANO:              Bergerac!
THE SENTRY ON THE PARAPET:         Halt!
               Who goes?—
CYRANO (*appears on the parapet*): Bergerac, idiot!
LE BRET (*goes to meet him*):       Thank God again!
CYRANO (*signs to him not to wake anyone*): Hush!
LE BRET:                 Wounded?—
CYRANO: No— They always miss me—quite
    A habit by this time!
LE BRET:         Yes— Go right on—
    Risk your life every morning before breakfast
    To send a letter!
CYRANO (*stops near* CHRISTIAN): I promised he should write
    Every single day . . .
    (*looks down at him*)    Hm— The boy looks pale
    When he is asleep—thin too—starving to death—
    If that poor child knew! Handsome, none the less . . .
LE BRET: Go and get some sleep!
CYRANO (*affectionately*):      Now, now—you old bear,
    No growling!—I am careful—you know I am—
    Every night, when I cross the Spanish lines
    I wait till they are all drunk.
LE BRET:            You might bring
    Something with you.
CYRANO:          I have to travel light
    To pass through— By the way, there will be news
    For you to-day: the French will eat or die,
    If what I saw means anything.

LE BRET:                          Tell us!
CYRANO:                                    No—
  I am not sure—we shall see!
CARBON:                          What a war,
  When the besieger starves to death!
LE BRET:                                    Fine war—
  Fine situation! We besiege Arras—
  The Cardinal Prince of Spain besieges us—
  And—here we are!
CYRANO:                Someone might besiege *him*.
CARBON: A hungry joke!
CYRANO:                Ho, ho!
LE BRET:                          Yes, you can laugh—
  Risking a life like yours to carry letters—
  Where are you going now?
CYRANO (*at the tent door*):      To write another.
    (*Goes into tent—*
    *A little more daylight. The clouds redden. The town of Arras*
    *shows on the horizon. A cannon shot is heard, followed*
    *immediately by a roll of drums, far away to the left. Other*
    *drums beat a little nearer. The drums go on answering each*
    *other here and there, approach, beat loudly almost on the*
    *stage, and die away toward the right, across the camp. The*
    *camp awakes. Voices of officers in the distance*)
CARBON (*sighs*):
  Those drums!—another good nourishing sleep
  Gone to the devil.
                (*The Cadets rouse themselves*)
         Now then!—
FIRST CADET (*sits up, yawns*):      God! I'm hungry!
SECOND CADET: Starving!
ALL (*groan*):          Aoh!
CARBON:                Up with you!
THIRD CADET:                          Not another step!
FOURTH CADET: Not another movement!

FIRST CADET:                              Look at my tongue—
    I said this air was indigestible!

FIFTH CADET: My coronet for half a pound of cheese!

SIXTH CADET:
    I have no stomach for this war— I'll stay
    In my tent—like Achilles.

ANOTHER:                        Yes—no bread,
    No fighting—

CARBON:          Cyrano!

OTHERS:                  May as well die—

CARBON:
    Come out here!—You know how to talk to them.
    Get them laughing—

SECOND CADET (*rushes up to* FIRST CADET *who is eating
    something*):          What are you gnawing there?

FIRST CADET:
    Gun wads and axle-grease. Fat country this
    Around Arras.

ANOTHER (*enters*): I have been out hunting!

ANOTHER (*enters*):                          I
    Went fishing, in the Scarpe!

ALL (*leaping up and surrounding the newcomers*):
                            Find anything?
    Any fish? Any game? Perch? Partridges?
    Let me look!

THE FISHERMAN: Yes—one gudgeon.          (*Shows it*)

THE HUNTER:                  One fat . . . sparrow.
    (*Shows it*)

ALL: Ah!—See here, this—mutiny!—

CARBON:                  Cyrano!
    Come and help!

CYRANO (*enters from tent*): Well?
    (*Silence. To the* FIRST CADET *who is walking away, with his
    chin on his chest*):          You there, with the long face?

FIRST CADET: I have something on my mind that troubles me.

CYRANO: What is that?

FIRST CADET:                My stomach.

CYRANO:                              So have I.

FIRST CADET:                              No doubt
    You enjoy this!

CYRANO (*tightens his belt*): It keeps me looking young.

SECOND CADET: My teeth are growing rusty.

CYRANO:                              Sharpen them!

THIRD CADET: My belly sounds as hollow as a drum.

CYRANO: Beat the long roll on it!

FOURTH CADET:                    My ears are ringing.

CYRANO: Liar! A hungry belly has no ears.

FIFTH CADET: Oh for a barrel of good wine!

CYRANO (*offers him his own helmet*):        Your casque.

SIXTH CADET: I'll swallow anything!

CYRANO (*throws him the book which he has in his hand*):
                              Try the "Iliad."

SEVENTH CADET:
    The Cardinal, he has four meals a day—
    What does he care!

CYRANO:              Ask him; he really ought
    To send you . . . a spring lamb out of his flock,
    Roasted whole—

THE CADET:        Yes, and a bottle—

CYRANO (*exaggerates the manner of one speaking to a servant*):
                              If you please,
    Richelieu—a little more of the Red Seal . . .
    Ah, thank you!

THE CADET:        And the salad—

CYRANO:                        Of course—Romaine!

ANOTHER CADET (*shivering*): I am as hungry as a wolf.

CYRANO (*tosses him a cloak*):              Put on
    Your sheep's clothing.

FIRST CADET (*with a shrug*): Always the clever answer!

CYRANO:
>     Always the answer—yes! Let me die so—
>     Under some rosy-golden sunset, saying
>     A good thing, for a good cause! By the sword,
>     The point of honour—by the hand of one
>     Worthy to be my foeman, let me fall—
>     Steel in my heart, and laughter on my lips!

VOICES HERE AND THERE: All very well— We are hungry!

CYRANO:                                             Bah! You think
>     Of nothing but yourselves.
>     (*his eye singles out the* OLD FIFER *in the background*)
>                                   Here, Bertrandou,
>     You were a shepherd once— Your pipe now! Come,
>     Breathe, blow,— Play to these belly-worshippers
>     The old airs of the South—
>                                   "Airs with a smile in them,
>     Airs with a sigh in them, airs with the breeze
>     And the blue of the sky in them—"
>                                             Small, demure tunes
>     Whose every note is like a little sister—
>     Songs heard only in some long silent voice
>     Not quite forgotten— Mountain melodies
>     Like thin smoke rising from brown cottages
>     In the still noon, slowly— Quaint lullabies,
>     Whose very music has a Southern tongue—
>             (THE OLD MAN *sits down and prepares his fife*)
>     Now let the fife, that dry old warrior,
>     Dream, while over the stops your fingers dance
>     A minuet of little birds—let him
>     Dream beyond ebony and ivory;
>     Let him remember he was once a reed
>     Out of the river, and recall the spirit
>     Of innocent, untroubled country days . . .
>             (THE FIFER *begins to play a Provençal melody*)
>     Listen, you Gascons! Now it is no more

The shrill fife— It is the flute, through woodlands far
Away, calling—no longer the hot battle-cry,
But the cool, quiet pipe our goatherds play!
Listen—the forest glens . . . the hills . . . the downs . . .
The green sweetness of night on the Dordogne . . .
Listen, you Gascons! It is all Gascoyne! . . .
(*Every head is bowed; every eye cast down. Here and there a tear is furtively brushed away with the back of a hand, the corner of a cloak*)

CARBON (*softly to* CYRANO): You make them weep—

CYRANO: For homesickness—a hunger
More noble than that hunger of the flesh;
It is their hearts now that are starving.

CARBON: Yes,
But you melt down their manhood.

CYRANO (*motions the drummer to approach*): You think so?
Let them be. There is iron in their blood
Not easily dissolved in tears. You need
Only— (*he makes a gesture; the drum beats*)

ALL (*spring up and rush toward their weapons*):
What's that? Where is it?—What?—

CYRANO (*smiles*): You see—
Let Mars snore in his sleep once—and farewell
Venus—sweet dreams—regrets—dear thoughts of home—
All the fife lulls to rest wakes at the drums!

A CADET (*looks upstage*): Aha— Monsieur de Guiche!

THE CADETS (*mutter among themselves*): Ugh! . . .

CYRANO (*smiles*) Flattering
Murmur!

A CADET: He makes me weary!

ANOTHER: With his collar
Of lace over his corselet—

ANOTHER: Like a ribbon
Tied round a sword!

ANOTHER:                    Bandages for a boil
On the back of his neck—
SECOND CADET:              A courtier always!
ANOTHER: The Cardinal's nephew!
CARBON:                    None the less—a Gascon.
FIRST CADET:
A counterfeit! Never you trust that man—
Because we Gascons, look you, are all mad—
This fellow is reasonable—nothing more
Dangerous than a reasonable Gascon!
LE BRET: He looks pale.
ANOTHER:                  Oh, he can be hungry too,
Like any other poor devil—but he wears
So many jewels on that belt of his
That his cramps glitter in the sun!
CYRANO (*quickly*):                  Is he
To see us looking miserable? Quick—
Pipes!—Cards!—Dice!—
(*They all hurriedly begin to play, on their stools, on the
drums, or on their cloaks spread on the ground, lighting their
long pipes meanwhile*)
As for me, I read Descartes.
(*He walks up and down, reading a small book which he takes
from his pocket. DE GUICHE enters, looking pale and
haggard. All are absorbed in their games. General air of
contentment. DE GUICHE goes to CARBON. They look at
each other askance, each observing with satisfaction the
condition of the other*)
DE GUICHE:
Good morning!
(*aside*)                  He looks yellow.
CARBON:                                    He is all eyes.
DE GUICHE (*looks at the Cadets*):
What have we here? Black looks? Yes, gentlemen—
I am informed I am not popular;

The hill-nobility, barons of Béarn,
The pomp and pride of Périgord—I learn
They disapprove their colonel; call him courtier,
Politician—they take it ill that I
Cover my steel with lace of Genoa.
It is a great offence to be a Gascon
And not to be a beggar!
(*Silence. They smoke. They play*)
                   Well— Shall I have
Your captain punish you? . . . No.

CARBON:
                      As to that,
It would be impossible.

DE GUICHE:         Oh?

CARBON:               I am free;
I pay my company; it is my own;
I obey military orders.

DE GUICHE:         Oh!
That will be quite enough.
(*To the Cadets*)      I can afford
Your little hates. My conduct under fire
Is well known. It was only yesterday
I drove the Count de Bucquoi from Bapaume,
Pouring my men down like an avalanche,
I myself led the charge—

CYRANO (*without looking up from his book*):
                And your white scarf?

DE GUICHE (*surprised and gratified*):
You heard that episode? Yes—rallying
My men for the third time, I found myself
Carried among a crowd of fugitives
Into the enemy's lines. I was in danger
Of being shot or captured; but I thought
Quickly—took off and flung away the scarf
That marked my military rank—and so
Being inconspicuous, escaped among

My own force, rallied them, returned again
And won the day! . . .
(*The Cadets do not appear to be listening, but here and there
the cards and the dice boxes remain motionless, the smoke is
retained in their cheeks*)

                    What do you say to that?
Presence of mind—yes?

CYRANO:              Henry of Navarre
Being outnumbered, never flung away
His white plume.
(*Silent enjoyment. The cards flutter, the dice roll, the smoke
puffs out*)

DE GUICHE:      My device was a success.    However!
(*Same attentive pause, interrupting the games and the smoking*)

CYRANO:      Possibly . . . An officer
Does not lightly resign the privilege
Of being a target.
(*Cards, dice, and smoke fall, roll, and float away with
increasing satisfaction*)

                    Now, if I had been there—
Your courage and my own differ in this—
When your scarf fell, I should have put it on.

DE GUICHE: Boasting again!

CYRANO:             Boasting? Lend it to me
To-night; I'll lead the first charge, with your scarf
Over my shoulder!

DE GUICHE:       Gasconnade once more!
You are safe making that offer, and you know it—
My scarf lies on the river bank between
The lines, a spot swept by artillery
Impossible to reach alive!

CYRANO (*produces the scarf from his pocket*):
                    Yes. Here . . .
(*Silence. The Cadets stifle their laughter behind their cards
and their dice boxes. DE GUICHE turns to look at them.*

*Immediately they resume their gravity and their game. One of them whistles carelessly the mountain air which* THE FIFER *was playing*)

DE GUICHE (*takes the scarf*):

Thank you! That bit of white is what I need
To make a signal. I was hesitating—
You have decided me.

(*He goes up to the parapet, climbs upon it, and waves the scarf at arm's length several times*)

ALL:                                What is he doing?—
What?—

THE SENTRY ON THE PARAPET:

There's a man down there running away!

DE GUICHE (*descending*):

A Spaniard. Very useful as a spy
To both sides. He informs the enemy
As I instruct him. By his influence
I can arrange their dispositions.

CYRANO:                                Traitor!

DE GUICHE (*folding the scarf*):

A traitor, yes; but useful . . .

                                We were saying? . . .
Oh, yes— Here is a bit of news for you:
Last night we had hopes of reprovisioning
The army. Under cover of the dark,
The Marshal moved to Dourlens. Our supplies
Are there. He may reach them. But to return
Safely, he needs a large force—at least half
Our entire strength. At present, we have here
Merely a skeleton.

CARBON:                Fortunately,
The Spaniards do not know that.

DE GUICHE:                                Oh, yes; they know.
They will attack.

CARBON:                Ah!

5

DE GUICHE:                    From that spy of mine
    I learned of their intention. His report
    Will determine the point of their advance.
    The fellow asked me what to say! I told him:
    "Go out between the lines; watch for my signal;
    Where you see that, let them attack there."
CARBON (*to the Cadets*):                    Well,
    Gentlemen!
    (*All rise. Noise of sword belts and breastplates being buckled
    on*)
DE GUICHE:    You may have perhaps an hour.
FIRST CADET: Oh— An hour!
    (*They all sit down and resume their games once more*)
DE GUICHE (*to* CARBON):    The great thing is to gain time.
    Any moment the Marshal may return.
CARBON: And to gain time?
DE GUICHE:                    You will all be so kind
    As to lay down your lives!
CYRANO:                    Ah! Your revenge?
DE GUICHE:
    I make no great pretence of loving you!
    But—since you gentlemen esteem yourselves
    Invincible, the bravest of the brave,
    And all that—why need we be personal?
    I serve the king in choosing . . . as I choose!
CYRANO (*salutes*): Sir, permit me to offer—all our thanks.
DE GUICHE (*returns the salute*):
    You love to fight a hundred against one;
    Here is your opportunity!
    (*He goes upstage with* CARBON)
CYRANO (*to the Cadets*):        My friends,
    We shall add now to our old Gascon arms
    With their six chevrons, blue and gold, a seventh—
    Blood-red!
    (DE GUICHE *talks in a low tone to* CARBON *upstage.*

*Orders are given. The defence is arranged.* CYRANO *goes to* CHRISTIAN *who has remained motionless with folded arms)*
                Christian?          (*Lays a hand on his shoulder*)
CHRISTIAN (*shakes his head*): Roxane . . .
CYRANO:                              Yes.
CHRISTIAN:                                        I should like
    To say farewell to her, with my whole heart
    Written for her to keep.
CYRANO:                        I thought of that—
    (*Takes a letter from his doublet*)
    I have written your farewell.
CHRISTIAN:                          Show me!
CYRANO:                                            You wish
    To read it?
CHRISTIAN:      Of course!
    (*He takes the letter; begins to read, looks up suddenly*)
                        What?—
CYRANO:                        What is it?
CHRISTIAN:                                        Look—
    This little circle—
CYRANO (*takes back the letter quickly, and looks innocent*):
                        Circle?—
CHRISTIAN:                        Yes—a tear!
CYRANO:
    So it is! . . . Well—a poet while he writes
    Is like a lover in his lady's arms,
    Believing his imagination—all
    Seems true—you understand? There's half the charm
    Of writing— Now, this letter as you see
    I have made so pathetic that I wept
    While I was writing it!
CHRISTIAN:                You—wept?
CYRANO:                                    Why, yes—
    Because . . . it is a little thing to die,
    But—not to see her . . . that is terrible!

CYRANO: And I shall never—

>                                        (CHRISTIAN *looks at him*)
>                      We shall never—
>    (*Quickly*)                          You
>    Will never—

CHRISTIAN (*snatches the letter*): Give me that!
>    (*Noise in the distance on the outskirts of the camp*)

VOICE OF A SENTRY:                    Halt—who goes there?
>    (*Shots, shouting, jingle of harness*)

CARBON: What is it?—

THE SENTRY ON THE PARAPET: Why, a coach.
>    (*They rush to look*)

CONFUSED VOICES:                    What? In the Camp?
>    A coach? Coming this way— It must have driven
>    Through the Spanish lines—what the devil— Fire!—
>    No— Hark! The driver shouting—what does he say?
>    Wait— He said: "On the service of the King!"
>    (*They are all on the parapet looking over. The jingling comes
>    nearer*)

DE GUICHE: Of the King?
>    (*They come down and fall into line*)

CARBON:                    Hats off, all!

DE GUICHE (*speaks offstage*):                    The King! Fall in,
>    Rascals!—
>    (*The coach enters at full trot. It is covered with mud and dust.
>    The curtains are drawn. Two footmen are seated behind. It
>    stops suddenly*)

CARBON (*shouts*): Beat the assembly—
>    (*Roll of drums. All the Cadets uncover*)

DE GUICHE:                    Two of you,
>    Lower the steps—open the door—
>    (*Two men rush to the coach. The door opens*)

ROXANE (*comes out of the coach*):                    Good morning!
>    (*At the sound of a woman's voice, every head is raised.
>    Sensation*)

DE GUICHE: On the King's service— You?
ROXANE: Yes—my own king—
    Love!
CYRANO (*aside*): God is merciful . . .
CHRISTIAN (*hastens to her*): You! Why have you—
ROXANE: Your war lasted so long!
CHRISTIAN: But why?—
ROXANE: Not now—
CYRANO (*aside*): I wonder if I dare to look at her . . .
DE GUICHE: You cannot remain here!
ROXANE: Why, certainly!
    Roll that drum here, somebody . . .
    (*She sits on the drum which is brought to her*)
                      Thank you— There!
    (*She laughs*)
    Would you believe—they fired upon us?
                       —My coach
    Looks like the pumpkin in the fairy tale,
    Does it not? And my footmen—
    (*She throws a kiss to* CHRISTIAN) How do you do?
    (*She looks about*)
    How serious you all are! Do you know,
    It is a long drive here—from Arras?
    (*Sees* CYRANO) Cousin,
    I am glad to see you!
CYRANO (*advances*): Oh— How did you come?
ROXANE: How did I find you? Very easily—
    I followed where the country was laid waste
    —Oh, but I saw such things! I had to see
    To believe. Gentlemen, is that the service
    Of your King? I prefer my own!
CYRANO: But how
    Did you come through?
ROXANE: Why, through the Spanish lines
    Of course!

FIRST CADET:   They let you pass?—
DE GUICHE:                          What did you say?
    How did you manage?
LE BRET:                     Yes, that must have been
    Difficult!
ROXANE:       No— I simply drove along.
    Now and then some hidalgo scowled at me
    And I smiled back—my best smile; whereupon,
    The Spaniards being (without prejudice
    To the French) the most polished gentlemen
    In the world—I passed!
CARBON                        Certainly that smile
    Should be a passport! Did they never ask
    Your errand or your destination?
ROXANE:                        Oh,
    Frequently! Then I drooped my eyes and said:
    "I have a lover . . ." Whereupon, the Spaniard
    With an air of ferocious dignity
    Would close the carriage door—with such a gesture
    As any king might envy, wave aside
    The muskets that were levelled at my breast,
    Fall back three paces, equally superb
    In grace and gloom, draw himself up, thrust forth
    A spur under his cloak, sweeping the air
    With his long plumes, bow very low, and say:
    "Pass, Senorita!"
CHRISTIAN:            But Roxane—
ROXANE:                        I know—
    I said "a lover"—but you understand—
    Forgive me!—If I said "I am going to meet
    My husband," no one would believe me!
CHRISTIAN:                                Yes,
    But—
ROXANE:  What then?
DE GUICHE:           You must leave this place.

CYRANO:                                        At once.
ROXANE: I?
LE BRET:   Yes—immediately.
ROXANE:                        And why?  (*They are embarrassed*)
CHRISTIAN:                            Because . . .
CYRANO: In half an hour . . .
DE GUICHE:                  Or three quarters . . .
CARBON:                                        Perhaps
    It might be better . . .
LE BRET:                  If you . . .
ROXANE:                                Oh— I see!
    You are going to fight. I remain here.
ALL:                                        No—no!
ROXANE: He is my husband—
    (*Throws herself in* CHRISTIAN'S *arms*)
                      I will die with you!
CHRISTIAN: Your eyes! . . . Why do you?—
ROXANE:                                You know why . . .
DE GUICHE (*desperate*):                        This post
    Is dangerous—
ROXANE (*turns*):   How—dangerous?
CYRANO:                                The proof
    Is, we are ordered—
ROXANE (*to* DE GUICHE): Oh—you wish to make
    A widow of me?
DE GUICHE:            On my word of honour—
ROXANE:
    No matter. I am just a little mad—
    I will stay. It may be amusing.
CYRANO:                                What,
    A heroine—our intellectual?
ROXANE: Monsieur de Bergerac, I am your cousin!
A CADET: We'll fight now! Hurrah!
ROXANE (*more and more excited*):
                   I am safe with you—my friends!

ANOTHER (*carried away*):
　　The whole camp breathes of lilies!—
ROXANE:　　　　　　　　　　　　And I think,
　　This hat would look well on the battlefield! . . .
　　But perhaps—
　　(*looks at* DE GUICHE)
　　　　　　　　The Count ought to leave us. Any moment
　　Now, there may be danger.
DE GUICHE:　　　　　　　　　This is too much!
　　I must inspect my guns. I shall return—
　　You may change your mind— There will yet be time—
ROXANE: Never!
　　(DE GUICHE *goes out*)
CHRISTIAN (*imploring*): Roxane! . . .
ROXANE:　　　　　　　　　　　No!
FIRST CADET (*to the rest*):　　　　　She stays here!
ALL (*rushing about, elbowing each other, brushing off their clothes*):
　　　　　　　　　　　　　　　　　A comb!—
　　Soap!—Here's a hole in my— A needle!—Who
　　Has a ribbon?—Your mirror, quick!—My cuffs—
　　A razor—
ROXANE (*to* CYRANO, *who is still urging her*):
　　　　　　No! I shall not stir one step!
CARBON (*having, like the others, tightened his belt, dusted himself,
　　brushed off his hat, smoothed out his plume and put on his lace
　　cuffs, advances to* ROXANE *ceremoniously*):
　　In that case, may I not present to you
　　Some of these gentlemen who are to have
　　The honour of dying in your presence?
ROXANE (*bows*):　　　　　　　　　　Please!—
　　(*she waits, standing, on the arm of* CHRISTIAN, *while*
CARBON (*—presents*): Baron de Peyrescous de Colignac!
THE CADET (*salutes*): Madame . . .
ROXANE:　　　　　　　　　　　Monsieur . . .

CARBON (*continues*):                    Baron de Casterac
  De Cahuzac— Vidame de Malgouyre
  Estressac Lésbas d'Escarabiot—
THE VIDAME: Madame . . .
CARBON:                    Chevalier d'Antignac-Juzet—
  Baron Hillot de Blagnac-Saléchan
  De Castel-Crabioules—
THE BARON:               Madame . . .
ROXANE:                         How many
  Names you all have!
THE BARON:            Hundreds!
CARBON (*to* ROXANE):          Open the hand
  That holds your handkerchief.
ROXANE (*opens her hand; the handkerchief falls*): Why?
  (*The whole company makes a movement toward it*)
CARBON (*picks it up quickly*):              My company
  Was in want of a banner. We have now
  The fairest in the army!
ROXANE (*smiling*):          Rather small—
CARBON (*fastens the handkerchief to his lance*):
  Lace—and embroidered!
A CADET (*to the others*):      With her smiling on me,
  I could die happy, if I only had
  Something in my—
CARBON (*turns upon him*):      Shame on you! Feast your eyes
  And forget your—
ROXANE (*quickly*):      It must be this fresh air—
  I am starving! Let me see . . .

                              Cold partridges,
  Pastry, a little white wine—that would do.
  Will some one bring that to me?
A CADET (*aside*):              Will some one!—
ANOTHER: Where the devil are we to find—
ROXANE (*overhears; sweetly*):            Why, there—
  In my carriage.

ALL:                Wha-at?
ROXANE:                    All you have to do
    Is to unpack, and carve, and serve things.
                                    Oh,
    Notice my coachman; you may recognize
    An old friend.
THE CADETS (*rush to the coach*): Ragueneau!
ROXANE (*follows them with her eyes*):        Poor fellows . . .
THE CADETS (*acclamations*):        Ah!
    Ah!
CYRANO (*kisses her hand*): Our good fairy!
RAGUENEAU (*standing on his box, like a mountebank before a
    crowd*):                        Gentlemen!—
    (*Enthusiasm*)
THE CADETS:                            Bravo!
    Bravo!
RAGUENEAU: The Spaniards, basking in our smiles,
    Smiled on our baskets!                (*Applause*)
CYRANO (*aside, to* CHRISTIAN): Christian!—
RAGUENEAU:                        They adored
    The Fair, and missed—
    (*He takes from under the seat a dish, which he holds aloft*)
                            the Fowl!
    (*Applause. The dish is passed from hand to hand*)
CYRANO (*as before, to* CHRISTIAN):        One moment—
RAGUENEAU:                            Venus
    Charmed their eyes, while Adonis quietly
    (*Brandishing a ham*)
    Brought home the Boar!
    (*Applause; the ham is seized by a score of hands outstretched*)
CYRANO (*as before*):            Pst— Let me speak to you—
ROXANE (*as the Cadets return, their arms full of provisions*):
    Spread them out on the ground.
    (*Calls*)                        Christian! Come here;
    Make yourself useful.

(CHRISTIAN *turns to her, at the moment when* CYRANO *was leading him aside. She arranges the food, with his aid and that of the two imperturbable footmen*)

RAGUENEAU:                    Peacock, aux truffes!

FIRST CADET (*comes down, cutting a huge slice of the ham*):

                                                  Tonnerre!

We are not going to die without a gorge—
(*Sees* ROXANE; *corrects himself hastily*)
Pardon—a banquet!

RAGUENEAU (*tossing out the cushions of the carriage*):

                          Open these—they are full
Of ortolans!  (*Tumult; laughter; the cushions are eviscerated*)

THIRD CADET:   Lucullus!

RAGUENEAU (*throws out bottles of red wine*): Flasks of ruby—
(*and of white*)
Flasks of topaz—

ROXANE (*throws a tablecloth at the head of* CYRANO):

                    Come back out of your dreams!
Unfold this cloth—

RAGUENEAU (*takes off one of the lanterns of the carriage, and flourishes it*):            Our lamps are bonbonnières!

CYRANO (*to* CHRISTIAN):
I must see you before you speak with her—

RAGUENEAU (*more and more lyrical*):
My whip-handle is one long sausage!

ROXANE (*pouring wine; passing the food*):    We
Being about to die, first let us dine!
Never mind the others—all for Gascoyne!
And if De Guiche comes, he is not invited!
(*Going from one to another*)
Plenty of time—you need not eat so fast—
Hold your cup—
(*To another*)        What's the matter?

THE CADET (*sobbing*):                        You are so good
To us . . .

ROXANE:          There, there! Red or white wine?
                                    —Some bread
    For Monsieur de Carbon!—Napkins— A knife—
    Pass your plate— Some of the crust? A little more—
    Light or dark?—Burgundy?—
CYRANO (*follows her with an armful of dishes, helping to serve*):
                              Adorable!
ROXANE (*goes to* CHRISTIAN): What would you like?
CHRISTIAN:                                Nothing.
ROXANE:                      Oh, but you must!—
    A little wine? A biscuit?
CHRISTIAN:                Tell me first
    Why you came—
ROXANE:            By and by. I must take care
    Of these poor boys—
LE BRET (*who has gone upstage to pass up food to the sentry on the
    parapet, on the end of a lance*):
                        De Guiche!—
CYRANO:                        Hide everything
    Quick!—Dishes, bottles, tablecloth—
                              Now look
    Hungry again—
    (*To* RAGUENEAU) You there! Up on your box—
    —Everything out of sight?—
    (*In a twinkling, everything has been pushed inside the tents,
    hidden in their hats or under their cloaks.* DE GUICHE *enters
    quickly, then stops, sniffing the air. Silence*)
DE GUICHE:                  It smells good here.
A CADET (*humming with an air of great unconcern*):
                        Sing ha-ha-ha and ho-ho-ho—
DE GUICHE (*stares at him; he grows embarrassed*): You there—
    What are you blushing for?
THE CADET:                Nothing—my blood
    Stirs at the thought of battle.
ANOTHER:          Pom . . . pom . . . pom! . . .

DE GUICHE (*turns upon him*): What is that?

THE CADET (*slightly stimulated*):

       Only song—only little song—

DE GUICHE: You appear happy!

THE CADET:      Oh yes—always happy
  Before a fight—

DE GUICHE (*calls to* CARBON, *for the purpose of giving him an
  order*):    Captain! I—  (*stops and looks at him*)
           What the devil—
  You are looking happy too!—

CARBON (*pulls a long face and hides a bottle behind his back*):
         No!

DE GUICHE:       Here—I had
  One gun remaining. I have had it placed
  (*he points off-stage.*)
  There—in that corner—for your men.

A CADET (*simpering*):     *So kind!*—
  Charming attention!

ANOTHER:    Sweet solicitude!—

DE GUICHE (*contemptuous*): I believe you are both drunk—
  (*coldly*)       Being unaccustomed
  To guns—take care of the recoil!

FIRST CADET (*gesture*)    Ah-h . . . Pfft!

DE GUICHE (*goes up to him, furious*): How dare you?

FIRST CADET:   A Gascon's gun never recoils!

DE GUICHE (*shakes him by the arm*): You *are* drunk—

FIRST CADET (*superbly*):  With the smell of powder!

DE GUICHE (*turns away with a shrug*):   Bah!
  (*To* ROXANE) Madame, have you decided?

ROXANE:        I stay here.

DE GUICHE: You have time to escape—

ROXANE:      No!

DE GUICHE:      Very well—
  Someone give me a musket!

CARBON:     What?

DE GUICHE:                          *I stay*
    Here also.

CYRANO (*formally*): Sir, you show courage!

FIRST CADET:                        A Gascon
    In spite of all that lace!

ROXANE:                    Why—

DE GUICHE:                    Must I run
    Away, and leave a woman?

SECOND CADET (*to* FIRST CADET): We might give him
    Something to eat—what do you say?
    (*All the food reappears, as if by magic*)

DE GUICHE (*his face lights up*):        A feast!

THIRD CADET: Here a little, there a little—

DE GUICHE (*recovers his self-control; haughtily*):
                        Do you think
    I want your leavings?

CYRANO (*saluting*):        Colonel—you improve!

DE GUICHE: I can fight as I am!

FIRST CADET (*delighted*):        Listen to him—
    He has an accent!

DE GUICHE (*laughs*):   Have I so?

FIRST CADET:                    A Gascon!—
    A Gascon, after all!
    (*They all begin to dance*)

CARBON (*who has disappeared for a moment behind the parapet, reappears on top of it*): I have placed my pikemen
    Here.
    (*Indicates a row of pikes showing above the parapet*)

DE GUICHE (*bows to* ROXANE):
        We'll review them; will you take my arm?
    (*She takes his arm; they go up on the parapet. The rest uncover, and follow them upstage*)

CHRISTIAN (*goes hurriedly to* CYRANO): Speak quickly!
    (*At the moment when* ROXANE *appears on the parapet the pikes are lowered in salute, and a cheer is heard. She bows*)

THE PIKEMEN (*off-stage*): Hurrah!

CHRISTIAN: What is it?

CYRANO: If Roxane . . .

CHRISTIAN: Well?

CYRANO: Speaks about your letters . . .

CHRISTIAN: Yes—I know!

CYRANO: Do not make the mistake of showing . . .

CHRISTIAN: What?

CYRANO: Showing surprise.

CHRISTIAN: Surprise—why?

CYRANO: I must tell you! . . .
    It is quite simple—I had forgotten it
    Until just now. You have . . .

CHRISTIAN: Speak quickly!—

CYRANO: You
    Have written oftener than you think.

CHRISTIAN: Oh—have I!

CYRANO:
    I took upon me to interpret you;
    And wrote—sometimes . . . without . . .

CHRISTIAN: My knowing. Well?

CYRANO: Perfectly simple!

CHRISTIAN: Oh yes, perfectly!—
    For a month, we have been blockaded here!—
    How did you send all these letters?

CYRANO: Before
    Daylight, I managed—

CHRISTIAN: I see. That was also
    Perfectly simple!
                —So I wrote to her,
    How many times a week? Twice? Three times? Four?

CYRANO: Oftener.

CHRISTIAN: Every day?

CYRANO: Yes—every day . . .
    Every single day . . .

CHRISTIAN (*violently*):     And that wrought you up
　　Into such a flame that you faced death—
CYRANO (*sees* ROXANE *returning*):     Hush—
　　Not before her!
　　(*He goes quickly into the tent.* ROXANE *comes up to* CHRISTIAN)
ROXANE:     Now—Christian!
CHRISTIAN (*takes her hands*):     Tell me now
　　Why you came here—over these ruined roads—
　　Why you made your way among mosstroopers
　　And ruffians—you—to join me here?
ROXANE:     Because—
　　Your letters . . .
CHRISTIAN:     Meaning?
ROXANE:     It was your own fault
　　If I ran into danger! I went mad— .
　　Mad with you! Think what you have written me,
　　How many times, each one more wonderful
　　Than the last!
CHRISTIAN:     All this for a few absurd
　　Love-letters—
ROXANE:     Hush—absurd! How can you know?
　　I thought I loved you, ever since one night
　　When a voice that I never would have known
　　Under my window breathed your soul to me . . .
　　But—all this time, your letters—every one
　　Was like hearing your voice there in the dark,
　　All around me, like your arms around me . . .
　　(*more lightly*)     At last
　　I came. Anyone would! Do you suppose
　　The prim Penelope had stayed at home
　　Embroidering,—if Ulysses wrote like you?
　　She would have fallen like another Helen—
　　Tucked up those linen petticoats of hers
　　And followed him to Troy!
CHRISTIAN:     But you—

ROXANE:                         I read them
    Over and over. I grew faint reading them.
    I belonged to you. Every page of them
    Was like a petal fallen from your soul—
    Like the light and the fire of a great love,
    Sweet and strong and true—

CHRISTIAN:     Sweet . . . and strong . . . and true . . .
    You felt that, Roxane?—

ROXANE:                 You know how I feel! . . .

CHRISTIAN: So—you came . . .

ROXANE:               Oh my Christian, oh my king,—
    Lift me up if I fall upon my knees—
    It is the heart of me that kneels to you,
    And will remain forever at your feet—
    You cannot lift that!—
                   I came here to say
    'Forgive me'—(It is time to be forgiven
    Now, when we may die presently)—forgive me
    For being light and vain and loving you
    Only because you were beautiful.

CHRISTIAN (*astonished*):         Roxane! . . .

ROXANE:
    Afterwards I knew better. Afterwards
    (I had to learn to use my wings) I loved you
    For yourself too—knowing you more, and loving
    More of you. And now—

CHRISTIAN:          Now? . . .

ROXANE:               It is yourself
    I love now: your own self.

CHRISTIAN (*taken aback*):     Roxane!

ROXANE (*gravely*):            Be happy!—
    You must have suffered; for you must have seen
    How frivolous I was; and to be loved
    For the mere costume, the poor casual body
    You went about in—to a soul like yours,
    6

That must have been torture! Therefore with words
You revealed your heart. Now that image of you
Which filled my eyes first—I see better now,
And I see it no more!

CHRISTIAN:                    Oh!—

ROXANE:                              You still doubt
Your victory?

CHRISTIAN (*miserably*): Roxane!—

ROXANE:                              I understand:
You cannot perfectly believe in me—
A love like this—

CHRISTIAN:            I want no love like this!
I want love only for—

ROXANE:                    Only for what
Every woman sees in you? I can do
Better than that!

CHRISTIAN:          No—it was best before!

ROXANE:
You do not altogether know me . . . Dear,
There is more of me than there was—with this,
I can love more of you—more of what makes
You your own self—Truly! . . . If you were less
Lovable—

CHRISTIAN:    No!

ROXANE:            —Less charming—ugly even—
I should love you still.

CHRISTIAN:                You mean that?

ROXANE:                                  I do
Mean that!

CHRISTIAN:    Ugly? . . .

ROXANE:                    Yes. Even then!

CHRISTIAN (*agonized*):              Oh . . . God! . . .

ROXANE: Now are you happy?

CHRISTIAN (*choking*):        Yes . . .

ROXANE:                                What is it?

CHRISTIAN (*pushes her away gently*):          Only . . .
     Nothing . . . one moment . . .
ROXANE:                         But—
CHRISTIAN (*gesture toward the Cadets*):     I am keeping you
     From those poor fellows— Go and smile at them;
     They are going to die!
ROXANE (*softly*):          Dear Christian!
CHRISTIAN:                         Go—
     (*She goes up among the Gascons who gather round her
     respectfully*)
     Cyrano!
CYRANO (*comes out of the tent, armed for the battle*):
               What is wrong? You look—
CHRISTIAN:                         She does not
     Love me any more.
CYRANO (*smiles*):     You think not?
CHRISTIAN:                    She loves
     You.
CYRANO: No!—
CHRISTIAN (*bitterly*): She loves only my soul.
CYRANO:                         No!
CHRISTIAN:                         Yes—
     That means you. And you love her.
CYRANO:                    I?
CHRISTIAN:               I see—
     I know!
CYRANO:     That is true . . .
CHRISTIAN:          More than—
CYRANO (*quietly*):               More than that.
CHRISTIAN: Tell her so!
CYRANO:          No.
CHRISTIAN:     Why not?
CYRANO:               Why—look at me!
CHRISTIAN: She would love me if I were ugly.

CYRANO (*startled*):                              She—
    Said that?
CHRISTIAN:    Yes. Now then!
CYRANO (*half to himself*):        It was good of her
    To tell you that . . .
    (*change of tone*)        Nonsense! Do not believe
    Any such madness—
                        It was good of her
    To tell you. . . .
                    Do not take her at her word!
    Go on—you never will be ugly— Go!
    She would never forgive me.
CHRISTIAN:                          That is what
    We shall see.
CYRANO:          No, no—
CHRISTIAN:                    Let her choose between us!—
    Tell her everything!
CYRANO:                    No—you torture me—
CHRISTIAN:
    Shall I ruin your happiness, because
    I have a cursed pretty face? That seems
    Too unfair!
CYRANO:        And am I to ruin yours
    Because I happen to be born with power
    To say what you—perhaps—feel?
CHRISTIAN:                          Tell her!
CYRANO:                                  Man—
    Do not try me too far!
CHRISTIAN:                I am tired of being
    My own rival!
CYRANO:        Christian!—
CHRISTIAN:                    Our secret marriage—
    No witnesses—fraudulent—that can be
    Annulled—
CYRANO:        Do not try me—

CHRISTIAN:                    I want her love
    For the poor fool I am—or not at all!
    Oh, I am going through with this! I'll know,
    One way or the other. Now I shall walk down
    To the end of the post. Go tell her. Let her choose
    One of us.
CYRANO:    It will be you.
CHRISTIAN:                  God—I hope so!  (*He turns and calls*)
    Roxane!
CYRANO:   No—no—
ROXANE (*hurries down to him*): Yes, Christian?
CHRISTIAN:                              Cyrano
    Has news for you—important.
    (*She turns to* CYRANO. CHRISTIAN *goes out*)
ROXANE (*lightly*):                  Oh—important?
CYRANO: He is gone . . .
    (*To* ROXANE)          Nothing—only Christian thinks
    You ought to know—
ROXANE:                  I do know. He still doubts
    What I told him just now. I saw that.
CYRANO (*takes her hand*):          Was it
    True—what you told him just now?
ROXANE:                          It was true!
    I said that I should love him even . . .
CYRANO (*smiling sadly*):          The word
    Comes hard—before me?
ROXANE:                  Even if he were . . .
CYRANO:                          Say it—
    I shall not be hurt!—Ugly?
ROXANE:                  Even then
    I should love him.
    (*A few shots, off-stage, in the direction in which* CHRISTIAN
    *disappeared*)
          Hark! The guns—
CYRANO:                          Hideous?

ROXANE: Hideous.
CYRANO:          Disfigured?
ROXANE:                    Or disfigured.
CYRANO:                              Even
     Grotesque?
ROXANE:          How could he ever be grotesque—
     Ever—to me!
CYRANO:          But you could love him so,
     As much as?—
ROXANE:          Yes—and more!
CYRANO (*aside, excitedly*):          It is true!—true!—
     Perhaps—God! This is too much happiness . . .
     (*To* ROXANE)
     I—Roxane—listen—
LE BRET (*enters quickly; calls to* CYRANO *in a low tone*):
                    Cyrano—
CYRANO (*turns*):               Yes?
LE BRET:                    Hush! . . .
     (*Whispers a few words to him*)
CYRANO (*lets fall* ROXANE'S *hand*): Ah!
ROXANE:                    What is it?
CYRANO (*half stunned, and aside*):          All gone . . .
ROXANE (*more shots*): What is it? Oh,
     They are fighting!—
     (*She goes up to look off-stage*)
CYRANO:               All gone. I cannot ever
     Tell her, now . . . ever . . .
ROXANE (*starts to rush away*):     What has happened?
CYRANO (*restrains her*):               Nothing.
     (*Several Cadets enter. They conceal something which they are
     carrying, and form a group so as to prevent* ROXANE *from
     seeing their burden*)
ROXANE: These men—
CYRANO:          Come away . . .
     (*He leads her away from the group*)

ROXANE:                      You were telling me
     Something—
CYRANO:          Oh, that? Nothing. . . .
     (*gravely*)                     I swear to you
     That the spirit of Christian—that his soul
     Was—                 (*Corrects himself quickly*)
         That his soul is no less great—
ROXANE:                     Was?
     (*Crying out*)                 Oh!—
     (*She rushes among the men, and scatters them*)
CYRANO: All gone . . .
ROXANE (*sees* CHRISTIAN *lying upon his cloak*):
               Christian!
LE BRET (*to* CYRANO):          At the first volley.
     (ROXANE *throws herself upon the body of* CHRISTIAN. *Shots;*
     *at first scattered, then increasing. Drums. Voices shouting*)
CARBON (*sword in hand*):              Here
     They come!—Ready!—
     (*Followed by the Cadets, he climbs over the parapet and*
     *disappears*)
ROXANE:           Christian!
CARBON (*off-stage*):         Come on, there, You!
ROXANE: Christian!
CARBON:        Fall in!
ROXANE:          Christian!
CARBON:                 Measure your fuse!
     (RAGUENEAU *hurries up, carrying a helmet full of water*)
CHRISTIAN (*faintly*):         Roxane! . . .
CYRANO (*low and quick, in* CHRISTIAN'S *ear, while* ROXANE *is*
     *dipping into the water a strip of linen torn from her dress*):
               I have told her; she loves you.
     (CHRISTIAN *closes his eyes*)
ROXANE (*turns to* CHRISTIAN): Yes,
     My darling?
CARBON:        Draw your ramrods!

ROXANE (*to* CYRANO):                    He is not dead? . . .

CARBON: Open your charges!

ROXANE:                    I can feel his cheek
    Growing cold against mine—

CARBON:                    Take aim!

ROXANE:                         A letter—
    Over his heart—                    (*She opens it*)
         For me.

CYRANO (*aside*):              My letter . . .

CARBON:                         Fire!
    (*Musketry, cries and groans. Din of battle*)

CYRANO (*trying to withdraw his hand, which* ROXANE, *still upon
    her knees, is holding*):
    But Roxane—they are fighting—

ROXANE:                         Wait a little . . .
    He is dead. No one else knew him but you . . .
    (*She weeps quietly*)
    Was he not a great lover, a great man,
    A hero?

CYRANO (*standing, bareheaded*): Yes, Roxane.

ROXANE:                         A poet, unknown,
    Adorable?

CYRANO:        Yes, Roxane.

ROXANE:              A fine mind?

CYRANO: Yes, Roxane.

ROXANE:              A heart deeper than we knew—
    A soul magnificently tender?

CYRANO (*firmly*):                    Yes,
    Roxane!

ROXANE (*sinks down upon the breast of* CHRISTIAN):
        He is dead now . . .

CYRANO (*aside; draws his sword*):    Why, so am I—
    For I am dead, and my love mourns for me
    And does not know . . .         (*Trumpets in distance*)

DE GUICHE (*appears on the parapet, dishevelled, wounded on the*

*forehead, shouting*): The signal—hark—the trumpets!
The army has returned— Hold them now!—Hold
them!
The army!—

ROXANE: On his letter—blood . . . and tears.

A VOICE (*off-stage*): Surrender!

THE CADETS: No!

RAGUENEAU: This place is dangerous!—

CYRANO (*to* DE GUICHE): Take her away—I am going—

ROXANE (*kisses the letter; faintly*):
His blood . . . his tears . . .

RAGUENEAU (*leaps down from the coach and runs to her*):
She has fainted—

DE GUICHE (*on the parapet; savagely, to the Cadets*):
Hold them!

VOICE OFF-STAGE: Lay down your arms!

VOICES: No! No!

CYRANO (*to* DE GUICHE):
Sir, you have proved yourself— Take care of her.

DE GUICHE (*hurries to* ROXANE *and takes her up in his
arms*):
As you will—we can win, if you hold on
A little longer—

CYRANO: Good!
(*Calls out to* ROXANE, *as she is carried away, fainting, by*
DE GUICHE *and* RAGUENEAU):
Adieu, Roxane!
(*Tumult, outcries. Several Cadets come back wounded and fall
on the stage.* CYRANO, *rushing to the fight, is stopped on the
crest of the parapet by* CARBON, *covered with blood*)

CARBON: We are breaking—I am twice wounded—

CYRANO (*shouts to the Gascons*): Hardi!
Reculez pas, Drollos!
(*To* CARBON, *holding him up*) So—never fear!
I have two deaths to avenge now—Christian's

And my own!

(*They come down.* CYRANO *takes from him the lance with* ROXANE'S *handkerchief still fastened to it*)

    Float, little banner, with her name!

(*He plants it on the parapet; then shouts to the Cadets*)

Toumbé dessus! Escrasas lous!

(*To the fifer*)     Your fife!

Music!

(*Fife plays. The wounded drag themselves to their feet. Other Cadets scramble over the parapet and group themselves around* CYRANO *and his tiny flag. The coach is filled and covered with men, bristling with muskets, transformed into a redoubt*)

A CADET (*reels backward over the wall, still fighting. Shouts*):

   They are climbing over!—  (*and falls dead*)

CYRANO:       Very good—

Let them come!— A salute now—

(*The parapet is crowned for an instant with a rank of enemies. The imperial banner of Spain is raised aloft*) Fire!

(*General volley*)

VOICE (*among the ranks of the enemy*):   Fire!

(*murderous counter-fire; the Cadets fall on every side*)

A SPANISH OFFICER (*uncovers*):

Who are these men who are so fond of death?

CYRANO (*erect amid the hail of bullets, declaims*):

 The Cadets of Gascoyne, the defenders

  Of Carbon de Castel-Jaloux—

 Free fighters, free lovers, free spenders—

(*He rushes forward, followed by a few survivors*)

 The Cadets of Gascoyne . . .

*The rest is lost in the din of battle*


       CURTAIN

# ACT V

## CYRANO'S GAZETTE

*Fifteen years later, in 1655.* THE PARK OF THE CONVENT *occupied by the Ladies of the Cross, at Paris.*

*Magnificent foliage. To the left, the house upon a broad terrace at the head of a flight of steps, with several doors opening upon the terrace. In the centre of the scene an enormous tree alone in the centre of a little open space. Toward the right, in the foreground, among boxwood bushes, a semicircular bench of stone.*

*All the way across the background of the scene, an avenue over-arched by the chestnut trees, leading to the door of a chapel on the right, just visible among the branches of the trees. Beyond the double curtain of the trees, we catch a glimpse of bright lawns and shaded walks, masses of shrubbery; the perspective of the park; the sky.*

*A little side door of the chapel opens upon a colonnade, garlanded with autumnal vines, and disappearing on the right behind the box-trees.*

*It is late October. Above the still living green of the turf all the foliage is red and yellow and brown. The evergreen masses of box and yew stand out darkly against this autumnal colouring. A heap of dead leaves under every tree. The leaves are falling everywhere. They rustle underfoot along the walks; the terrace and the bench are half covered with them.*

*Before the bench on the right, on the side toward the tree, is placed a tall embroidery frame and beside it a little chair. Baskets filled with skeins of many-coloured silks and balls of wool. Tapestry unfinished on the frame.*

*At the Curtain Rise the nuns are coming and going across the park;*

*several of them are seated on the bench around* MOTHER MAR-
GUÉRITE DE JÉSUS. *The leaves are falling.*

SISTER MARTHE (*to* MOTHER MARGUÉRITE):
    Sister Claire has been looking in the glass
    At her new cap; twice!

MOTHER MARGUÉRITE (*to* SISTER CLAIRE):
                       It is very plain;
    Very.

SISTER CLAIRE: And Sister Marthe stole a plum
    Out of the tart this morning!

MOTHER MARGUÉRITE (*to* SISTER MARTHE):
                       That was wrong;
    Very wrong.

SISTER CLAIRE:    Oh, but such a little look!

SISTER MARTHE: Such a little plum!

MOTHER MARGUÉRITE (*severely*):     I shall tell Monsieur
    De Cyrano, this evening.

SISTER CLAIRE:              No! Oh, no!—
    He will make fun of us.

SISTER MARTHE:          He will say nuns
    Are so gay!

SISTER CLAIRE: And so greedy!

MOTHER MARGUÉRITE (*smiling*): And so good . . .

SISTER CLAIRE:
    It must be ten years, Mother Marguérite,
    That he has come here every Saturday,
    Is it not?

MOTHER MARGUÉRITE: More than ten years; ever since
    His cousin came to live among us here—
    Her worldly weeds among our linen veils,
    Her widowhood and our virginity—
    Like a black dove among white doves.

SISTER MARTHE:                 No one
    Else ever turns that happy sorrow of hers
    Into a smile.

ALL THE NUNS:  He is such fun!—He makes us
    Almost laugh!—And he teases everyone—
    And pleases everyone— And we all love him—
    And he likes our cake, too—
SISTER MARTHE:                    I am afraid
    He is not a good Catholic.
SISTER CLAIRE:                    Some day
    We shall convert him.
THE NUNS:                    Yes—yes!
MOTHER MARGUÉRITE:                    Let him be;
    I forbid you to worry him. Perhaps
    He might stop coming here.
SISTER MARTHE:                    But . . . God?
MOTHER MARGUÉRITE:                    You need not
    Be afraid. God knows all about him.
SISTER MARTHE:                    Yes . . .
    But every Saturday he says to me,
    Just as if he were proud of it: "Well, Sister,
    I ate meat yesterday!"
MOTHER MARGUÉRITE:    He tells you so?
    The last time he said that, he had not eaten
    Anything, for two days.
SISTER MARTHE:                    Mother!—
MOTHER MARGUÉRITE:                    He is poor;
    Very poor.
SISTER MARTHE: Who said so?
MOTHER MARGUÉRITE:                    Monsieur Le Bret.
SISTER MARTHE: Why does not someone help him?
MOTHER MARGUÉRITE:                    He would be
    Angry; very angry . . .
    (*Between the trees upstage*, ROXANE *appears, all in black,
    with a widow's cap and long veils.* DE GUICHE, *magnificently
    grown old, walks beside her. They move slowly.* MOTHER
    MARGUÉRITE *rises*)          Let us go in—
    Madame Madeleine has a visitor.

SISTER MARTHE (*to* SISTER CLAIRE):
>    The Duc de Grammont, is it not? The Marshal?
SISTER CLAIRE (*looks toward* DE GUICHE):
>    I think so—yes.
SISTER MARTHE:        He has not been to see her
>    For months—
THE NUNS:            He is busy—the Court!—the Camp!—
SISTER CLAIRE:                        The world! . . .
>    (*They go out.* DE GUICHE *and* ROXANE *come down in
>    silence, and stop near the embroidery frame. Pause*)
DE GUICHE:
>    And you remain here, wasting all that gold—
>    For ever in mourning?
ROXANE:                    For ever.
DE GUICHE:                        And still faithful?
ROXANE: And still faithful . . .
DE GUICHE (*after a pause*):    Have you forgiven me?
ROXANE (*simply, looking up at the cross of the Convent*):
>    I am here.                    (*Another pause*)
DE GUICHE:  Was Christian . . . all that?
ROXANE:                            If you knew him.
DE GUICHE:
>    Ah? We were not precisely . . . intimate . . .
>    And his last letter—always at your heart?
ROXANE: It hangs here, like a holy reliquary.
DE GUICHE: Dead—and you love him still!
ROXANE:                            Sometimes I think
>    He has not altogether died; our hearts
>    Meet, and his love flows all around me, living.
DE GUICHE (*after another pause*): You see Cyrano often?
ROXANE:                            Every week.
>    My old friend takes the place of my Gazette,
>    Brings me all the news. Every Saturday,
>    Under that tree where you are now, his chair
>    Stands, if the day be fine. I wait for him,

Embroidering; the hour strikes; then I hear,
(I need not turn to look!) at the last stroke,
His cane tapping the steps. He laughs at me
For my eternal needlework. He tells
The story of the past week—
(LE BRET *appears on the steps*)
              There's Le Bret!—
(LE BRET *approaches*)
How is it with our friend?

LE BRET:           Badly.

DE GUICHE:           Indeed?

ROXANE (*to* DE GUICHE):
          Oh, he exaggerates!

LE BRET:           Just as I said—
Loneliness, misery—I told him so!—
His satires make a host of enemies—
He attacks the false nobles, the false saints,
The false heroes, the false artists—in short,
Everyone!

ROXANE:    But they fear that sword of his—
No one dare touch him!

DE GUICHE (*with a shrug*):   H'm—that may be so.

LE BRET:
It is not violence I fear for him,
But solitude—poverty—old grey December,
Stealing on wolf's feet, with a wolf's green eyes,
Into his darkening room. Those bravoes yet
May strike our Swordsman down! Every day now,
He draws his belt up one hole; his poor nose
Looks like old ivory; he has one coat
Left—his old black serge.

DE GUICHE:        That is nothing strange
In this world! No, you need not pity him
Overmuch.

LE BRET (*with a bitter smile*): My lord Marshal! . . .

DE GUICHE:                                    I say do not
      Pity him overmuch. He lives his life,
      His own life, his own way—thought, word, and deed
      Free!
LE BRET (*as before*): My lord Duke! . . .
DE GUICHE (*haughtily*):            Yes, I know—I have all;
      He has nothing. Nevertheless, to-day
      I should be proud to shake his hand . . .
      (*Saluting* ROXANE)                    Adieu.
ROXANE: I will go with you.
      (DE GUICHE *salutes* LE BRET, *and turns with* ROXANE
      *toward the steps*)
DE GUICHE (*pauses on the steps, as she climbs*):
                              Yes— I envy him
      Now and then . . .
                              Do you know, when a man wins
      Everything in this world, when he succeeds
      Too much—he feels, having done nothing wrong
      Especially, Heaven knows!—he feels somehow
      A thousand small displeasures with himself,
      Whose whole sum is not quite Remorse, but rather
      A sort of vague disgust . . . The ducal robes
      Mounting up, step by step, to pride and power,
      Somewhere among their folds draw after them
      A rustle of dry illusions, vain regrets,
      As your veil, up the stairs here, draws along
      The whisper of dead leaves.
ROXANE (*ironical*):            The sentiment
      Does you honour.
DE GUICHE:        Oh, yes . . .        (*pausing suddenly*)
                              Monsieur Le Bret!—
      (*To* ROXANE) You pardon us?—
      (*He goes to* LE BRET, *and speaks in a low tone*)
                              One moment— It is true
      That no one dares attack your friend. Some people

Dislike him, none the less. The other day
At Court, such a one said to me: "This man
Cyrano may die—accidentally."
LE BRET (*coldly*): Thank you.
DE GUICHE:          You may thank me. Keep him at home
All you can. Tell him to be careful.
LE BRET (*shaking his hands to heaven*):   Careful!—
He is coming here. I'll warn him—yes, but! . . .
ROXANE (*still on the steps, to* A NUN *who approaches her*):
                                                      Here
I am—what is it?
THE NUN:          Madame, Ragueneau
Wishes to see you.
ROXANE:          Bring him here.
(*To* LE BRET *and* DE GUICHE)     He comes
For sympathy—having been first of all
A Poet, he became since then, in turn,
A Singer—
LE BRET:     Bath-house keeper—
ROXANE:               Sacristan—
LE BRET: Actor—
ROXANE:          Hairdresser—
LE BRET:               Music-master—
ROXANE:                         Now,
To-day—
RAGUENEAU (*enters hurriedly*): Madame!—
(*He sees* LE BRET)               Monsieur!—
ROXANE (*smiling*):               First tell your troubles
To Le Bret for a moment.
RAGUENEAU:               But Madame—
(*She goes out, with* DE GUICHE, *not hearing him.* RAGUENEAU
*comes to* LE BRET)
After all, I had rather— You are here—
She need not know so soon— I went to see him
Just now— Our friend— As I came near his door,

I saw him coming out. I hurried on
To join him. At the corner of the street,
As he passed— Could it be an accident?—
I wonder!—At the window overhead,
A lackey with a heavy log of wood
Let it fall—

LE BRET: Cyrano!

RAGUENEAU: I ran to him—

LE BRET: God! The cowards!

RAGUENEAU: I found him lying there—
A great hole in his head—

LE BRET: Is he alive?

RAGUENEAU:
Alive—yes. But . . . I had to carry him
Up to his room—Dieu! Have you seen his room?—

LE BRET: Is he suffering?

RAGUENEAU: No; unconscious.

LE BRET: Did you
Call a doctor?

RAGUENEAU: One came—for charity.

LE BRET: Poor Cyrano!—We must not tell Roxane
All at once . . . Did the doctor say?—

RAGUENEAU: He said
Fever, and lesions of the— I forget
Those long names— Ah, if you had seen him there,
His head all white bandages!—Let us go
Quickly—there is no one to care for him—
All alone— If he tries to raise his head,
He may die!

LE BRET (*draws him away to the right*):
This way— It is shorter—through
The Chapel—

ROXANE (*appears on the stairway, and calls to* LE BRET *as he is
going out by the colonnade which leads to the small door of the
Chapel*): Monsieur Le Bret!—

(Le Bret *and* Ragueneau *rush off without hearing*)
                                        Running away
When I call to him? Poor dear Ragueneau
Must have been very tragic!
(*She comes slowly down the stair, toward the tree*)
                                        What a day! . . .
Something in these bright Autumn afternoons
Happy and yet regretful—an old sorrow
Smiling . . . as though poor little April dried
Her tears long ago—and remembered . . .
(*She sits down at her work. Two nuns come out of the house
carrying a great chair and set it under the tree*)          Ah—
The old chair, for my old friend!—

SISTER MARTHE:                          The best one
In our best parlour!—

ROXANE:                          Thank you, Sister—
(*The nuns withdraw*)
                                                There—
(*she begins embroidering. The clock strikes*)
The hour!—He will be coming now—my silks—
All done striking? He never was so late
Before! The sister at the door—my thimble . . .
Here it is—she must be exhorting him
To repent all his sins . . .                    (*A pause*)
                          He ought to be
Converted, by this time— Another leaf—
(*A dead leaf falls on her work; she brushes it away*)
Certainly nothing could—my scissors—ever
Keep him away—

A NUN (*appears on the steps*): Monsieur de Bergerac.

ROXANE (*without turning*):
What was I saying? . . . Hard, sometimes, to match
These faded colours! . . .
(*While she goes on working,* CYRANO *appears at the top of
the steps, very pale, his hat drawn over his eyes.* THE NUN

*who has brought him in goes away. He begins to descend the steps leaning on his cane, and holding himself on his feet only by an evident effort.* ROXANE *turns to him, with a tone of friendly banter*)　　　After fourteen years,
　　Late—for the first time!

CYRANO (*reaches the chair, and sinks into it; his gay tone contrasting with his tortured face*):
　　　　　　　　　　Yes, yes—maddening!
　　I was detained by—

ROXANE:　　　　Well?

CYRANO:　　　　　A visitor,
　　Most unexpected.

ROXANE (*carelessly, still sewing*): Was your visitor
　　Tiresome?

CYRANO:　　Why, hardly that—inopportune,
　　Let us say—an old friend of mine—at least
　　A very old acquaintance.

ROXANE:　　　　　　Did you tell him
　　To go away?

CYRANO:　　　For the time being, yes.
　　I said: "Excuse me—this is Saturday—
　　I have a previous engagement, one
　　I cannot miss, even for you— Come back
　　An hour from now."

ROXANE:　　　　　　Your friend will have to wait;
　　I shall not let you go till dark.

CYRANO (*very gently*):　　　Perhaps
　　A little before dark, I must go . . .
　　(*He leans back in the chair, and closes his eyes.* SISTER MARTHE *crosses above the stairway.* ROXANE *sees her, motions her to wait, then turns to* CYRANO)

ROXANE:　　　　　　　Look—
　　Somebody waiting to be teased.

CYRANO (*quickly, opens his eyes*):　　Of course!
　　(*In a big, comic voice*)

Sister, approach!
(SISTER MARTHE *glides toward him*)
               Beautiful downcast eyes!—
So shy—
SISTER MARTHE (*looks up, smiling*): You—
   (*She sees his face*)           Oh!—
CYRANO (*indicates* ROXANE):       Sh!—Careful!
   (*Resumes his burlesque tone*)      Yesterday,
I ate meat again!
SISTER MARTHE:    Yes, I know.
   (*Aside*)             That is why
He looks so pale . . .
   (*To him: low and quickly*) In the refectory,
Before you go—come to me there—
                      I'll make you
A great bowl of hot soup—will you come?
CYRANO (*boisterously*):         Ah—
Will I come!
SISTER MARTHE: You are quite reasonable
To-day!
ROXANE:    Has she converted you?
SISTER MARTHE:         Oh, no—
Not for the world!—
CYRANO           Why, now I think of it,
That is so— You, bursting with holiness,
And yet you never preach! Astonishing
I call it . . .
   (*With burlesque ferocity*)   Ah—now I'll astonish you—
I am going to—
   (*With the air of seeking for a good joke and finding it*)
            —let you pray for me
To-night, at vespers!
ROXANE:        Aha!
CYRANO:          Look at her—
Absolutely struck dumb!

SISTER MARTHE (*gently*):       I did not wait
    For you to say I might.                    (*She goes out*)
CYRANO (*returns to* ROXANE, *who is bending over her work*):
                              Now, may the devil
    Admire me, if I ever hope to see
    The end of that embroidery!
ROXANE (*smiling*):              I thought
    It was time you said that.
    (*A breath of wind causes a few leaves to fall*)
CYRANO:                        The leaves—
ROXANE (*raises her head and looks away through the trees*):
                              What colour—
    Perfect Venetian red! Look at them fall.
CYRANO: Yes—they know how to die. A little way
    From the branch to the earth, a little fear
    Of mingling with the common dust—and yet
    They go down gracefully—a fall that seems
    Like flying!
ROXANE:        Melancholy—you?
CYRANO:                        Why, no,
    Roxane!
ROXANE:     Then let the leaves fall. Tell me now
    The Court news—my gazette!
CYRANO:                        Let me see—
ROXANE:                              Ah!
CYRANO (*more and more pale, struggling against pain*):
    Saturday, the nineteenth: The King fell ill,
    After eight helpings of grape marmalade.
    His malady was brought before the court,
    Found guilty of high treason; whereupon
    His Majesty revived. The royal pulse
    Is now normal. Sunday, the twentieth:
    The Queen gave a grand ball, at which they burned
    Seven hundred and sixty-three wax candles. Note:
    They say our troops have been victorious

In Austria. Later: Three sorcerers
Have been hung. Special post: The little dog
Of Madame d'Athis was obliged to take
Four pills before—

ROXANE:                    Monsieur de Bergerac,
Will you kindly be quiet!

CYRANO:                         Monday . . . nothing.
Lygdamire has a new lover.

ROXANE:                              Oh!

CYRANO (*his face more and more altered*): Tuesday,
The Twenty-second: All the court has gone
To Fontainebleau. Wednesday: The Comte de Fiesque
Spoke to Madame de Montglat; she said No.
Thursday: Mancini was the Queen of France
Or—very nearly! Friday: La Montglat
Said Yes. Saturday, twenty-sixth. . . .
(*His eyes close; his head sinks back; silence*)

ROXANE (*surprised at not hearing any more, turns, looks at him,
and rises, frightened*):                    He has fainted—
(*She runs to him, crying out*)
Cyrano!

CYRANO (*opens his eyes*): What . . . What is it? . . .
(*He sees* ROXANE *leaning over him, and quickly pulls his hat
down over his head and leans back away from her in the chair*)
                                   No—oh no—

It is nothing—truly!

ROXANE:                    But—

CYRANO:                         My old wound—
At Arras—sometimes—you know. . . .

ROXANE:                                   My poor friend!

CYRANO: Oh, it is nothing; it will soon be gone. . . .
                                   (*forcing a smile*)

There! It is gone!

ROXANE (*standing close to him*):
                    We all have our old wounds—

I have mine—here . . .              (*her hand at her breast*)
                              under this faded scrap
Of writing. . . . It is hard to read now—all
But the blood—and the tears. . . .
(*Twilight begins to fall*)

CYRANO:                              His letter! . . . Did you
    Not promise me that some day . . . that some day . . .
    You would let me read it?

ROXANE:                              His letter?—You . . .
    You wish—

CYRANO:        I do wish it—to-day.

ROXANE (*gives him the little silken bag from around her neck*):
                              Here. . . .

CYRANO: May I . . . open it?

ROXANE:                    Open it, and read.
    (*She goes back to her work, folds it again, rearranges her
    silks*)

CYRANO (*unfolds the letter; reads*):
    "Farewell Roxane, because to-day I die—"

ROXANE (*looks up, surprised*): Aloud?

CYRANO (*reads*):                "I know that it will be to-day,
    My own dearly beloved—and my heart
    Still so heavy with love I have not told,
    And I die without telling you! No more
    Shall my eyes drink the sight of you like wine,
    Never more, with a look that is a kiss,
    Follow the sweet grace of you—"

ROXANE:                              How you read it—
    His letter!

CYRANO (*continues*): "I remember now the way
    You have, of pushing back a lock of hair
    With one hand, from your forehead—and my heart
    Cries out—"

ROXANE:        His letter . . . and you read it so . . .
    (*The darkness increases imperceptibly*)

CYRANO:

"Cries out and keeps crying: 'Farewell, my dear,
My dearest—' "

ROXANE:          In a voice. . . .

CYRANO:                    "—My own heart's own,
My own treasure—"

ROXANE (*dreamily*):      In such a voice. . . .

CYRANO:                    —"My love—"

ROXANE: —As I remember hearing . . .
(*She trembles*)          —long ago. . . .
(*She comes near him, softly, without his seeing her; passes the
chair, leans over silently, looking at the letter. The darkness
increases*)

CYRANO:

"—I am never away from you. Even now,
I shall not leave you. In another world,
I shall be still that one who loves you, loves you
Beyond measure, beyond—"

ROXANE (*lays her hand on his shoulder*): How can you read
Now? It is dark. . . .
(*He starts, turns, and sees her there close to him. A little
movement of surprise, almost of fear; then he bows his head.
A long pause; then in the twilight now completely fallen, she
says very softly, clasping her hands*):
                    And all these fourteen years,
He has been the old friend, who came to me
To be amusing.

CYRANO:          Roxane!—

ROXANE:              It was you.

CYRANO: No, no, Roxane, no!

ROXANE:              And I might have known,
Every time that I heard you speak my name! . . .

CYRANO: No— It was not I—

ROXANE:              It was . . . you!

CYRANO:                    I swear—

ROXANE: I understand everything now: The letters—
    That was you . . .
CYRANO:                    No!
ROXANE:                            And the dear, foolish words—
    That was you. . . .
CYRANO:                   No!
ROXANE:                          And the voice . . . in the dark. . . .
    That was . . . you!
CYRANO:                  On my honour—
ROXANE:                                And . . . the Soul!—
    That was all you.
CYRANO:                 I never loved you—
ROXANE:                                      Yes,
    You loved me.
CYRANO (*desperately*): No— He loved you—
ROXANE:                                    Even now,
    You love me!
CYRANO (*his voice weakens*): No!
ROXANE (*smiling*):        And why . . . so great a "No"?
CYRANO: No, no, my own dear love, I love you not! . . .
    (*Pause*)
ROXANE:
    How many things have died . . . and are new-
        born! . . .
    Why were you silent for so many years,
    All the while, every night and every day,
    He gave me nothing—you knew that— You knew
    Here, in this letter lying on my breast,
    Your tears— You knew they were your tears—
CYRANO (*holds the letter out to her*):            The blood
    Was his.
ROXANE:     Why do you break that silence now,
    To-day?
CYRANO:    Why? Oh, because—
    (LE BRET *and* RAGUENEAU *enter, running*)

LE BRET:                   What recklessness—
    I knew it! He is here!

CYRANO (*smiling, and trying to rise*): Well? Here I am!

RAGUENEAU: He has killed himself, Madame, coming here!

ROXANE:
    He— Oh, God! . . . And that faintness . . . was that?—

CYRANO:       No,
    Nothing! I did not finish my Gazette—
    Saturday, twenty-sixth: An hour or so
    Before dinner, Monsieur de Bergerac
    Died, foully murdered.
    (*He uncovers his head, and shows it swathed in bandages*)

ROXANE:   .             Oh, what does he mean?—
    Cyrano!—What have they done to you?—

CYRANO:                   "Struck down
    By the sword of a hero, let me fall—
    Steel in my heart, and laughter on my lips!"
    Yes, I said that once. How Fate loves a jest!—
    Behold me ambushed—taken in the rear—
    My battlefield a gutter—my noble foe
    A lackey, with a log of wood! . . .
                       It seems
    Too logical— I have missed everything,
    Even my death!

RAGUENEAU (*breaks down*): Ah, monsieur!—

CYRANO:                  Ragueneau,
    Stop blubbering!
    (*Takes his hand*) What are you writing nowadays,
    Old poet?

RAGUENEAU (*through his tears*): I am not a poet now;
    I snuff the—light the candles—for Molière!

CYRANO: Oh—Molière!

RAGUENEAU:       Yes, but I am leaving him
    To-morrow. Yesterday they played "Scapin"—
    He has stolen your scene—

LE BRET:                    The whole scene—word for word!

RAGUENEAU: Yes: "What the devil was he doing there"—
That one!

LE BRET (*furious*): And Molière stole it all from you—
Bodily!—

CYRANO:          Bah— He showed good taste. . . .
(*To* RAGUENEAU)                              The Scene
Went well? . . .

RAGUENEAU    Ah, monsieur, they laughed—and laughed—
How they did laugh!

CYRANO:                    Yes—that has been my life. . . .
Do you remember that night Christian spoke
Under your window? It was always so!
While I stood in the darkness underneath,
Others climbed up to win the applause—the kiss!—
Well—that seems only justice— I still say,
Even now, on the threshold of my tomb—
"Molière has genius—Christian had good looks—"
(*The chapel bell is ringing. Along the avenue of trees above the
stairway, the nuns pass in procession to their prayers*)
They are going to pray now; there is the bell.

ROXANE (*raises herself and calls to them*):
Sister!—Sister!—

CYRANO (*holding on to her hand*): No,—do not go away—
I may not still be here when you return. . . .
(*The nuns have gone into the chapel. The organ begins to play*)
A little harmony is all I need—
Listen. . . .

ROXANE:          You shall not die! I love you!—

CYRANO:                                        No—
That is not in the story! You remember
When Beauty said "I love you" to the Beast
That was a fairy prince, his ugliness
Changed and dissolved, like magic. . . . But you see
I am still the same.

ROXANE:                    And I—I have done
     This to you! All my fault—mine!
CYRANO:                                You? Why no,
     On the contrary! I had never known
     Womanhood and its sweetness but for you.
     My mother did not love to look at me—
     I never had a sister— Later on,
     I feared the mistress with a mockery
     Behind her smile. But you—because of you
     I have had one friend not quite all a friend—
     Across my life, one whispering silken gown! . . .
LE BRET (*points to the rising moon which begins to shine down
     between the trees*):
     Your other friend is looking at you.
CYRANO (*smiling at the moon*):              I see. . . .
ROXANE:
     I never loved but one man in my life,
     And I have lost him—twice. . . .
CYRANO:
     Le Bret—I shall be up there presently
     In the moon—without having to invent
     Any flying machines!
ROXANE:                    What are you saying? . . .
CYRANO:
     The moon—yes, that would be the place for me—
     My kind of paradise! I shall find there
     Those other souls who should be friends of mine—
     Socrates—Galileo—
LE BRET (*revolting*):      No! No! No!
     It is too idiotic—too unfair—
     Such a friend—such a poet—such a man
     To die so—to die so!—
CYRANO (*affectionately*):      There goes Le Bret,
     Growling!
LE BRET (*breaks down*): My friend!—

CYRANO (*half raises himself, his eye wanders*):

                        The Cadets of Gascoyne,
  The Defenders. . . . The elementary mass—
  Ah—there's the point! Now, then . . .

LE BRET:                              Delirious—
  And all that learning—

CYRANO:                On the other hand,
  We have Copernicus—

ROXANE:                Oh!

CYRANO (*more and more delirious*): "Very well,
  But what the devil was he doing there?—
  What the devil was he doing there, up there?" . . .
  (*He declaims*)

      Philosopher and scientist,
      Poet, musician, duellist—
        He flew high, and fell back again!
      A pretty wit—whose like we lack—
      A lover . . . not like other men. . . .
        Here lies Hercule-Savinien
      De Cyrano de Bergerac—
        Who was all things—and all in vain!

  Well, I must go—pardon— I cannot stay!
  My moonbeam comes to carry me away. . . .
  (*He falls back into the chair, half fainting. The sobbing of
  ROXANE recalls him to reality. Gradually his mind comes
  back to him. He looks at her, stroking the veil that hides her
  hair*)
  I would not have you mourn any the less
  That good, brave, noble Christian; but perhaps—
  I ask you only this—when the great cold
  Gathers around my bones, that you may give
  A double meaning to your widow's weeds
  And the tears you let fall for him may be
  For a little—my tears. . . .

ROXANE (*sobbing*):           Oh, my love! . . .

CYRANO (*suddenly shaken as with a fever fit, he raises himself erect and pushes her away*):          —Not here!—
Not lying down! . . .
(*They spring forward to help him; he motions them back*)
                    Let no one help me—no one!—
Only the tree. . . .
(*He sets his back against the trunk. Pause*)
                    It is coming . . . I feel
Already shod with marble . . . gloved with lead . . .
(*Joyously*)
Let the old fellow come now! He shall find me
On my feet—sword in hand—          (*draws his sword*)

LE BRET:                    Cyrano!—

ROXANE (*half fainting*):                    Oh,
Cyrano!

CYRANO:     I can see him there—he grins—
He is looking at my nose—that skeleton
—What's that you say? Hopeless?—Why, very well!
But a man does not fight merely to win!
No—no—better to know one fights in vain! . . .
You there— Who are you? A hundred against one—
I know them now, my ancient enemies—
(*He lunges at the empty air*)
Falsehood!   . . .   There!   There!   Prejudice—
     Compromise—
Cowardice—
(*Thrusting*)   What's that? No! Surrender? No!
Never—never! . . .
                    Ah, you too, Vanity!
I knew you would overthrow me in the end—
No! I fight on! I fight on! I fight on!
(*He swings the blade in great circles, then pauses, gasping.
When he speaks again, it is in another tone*)
Yes, all my laurels you have riven away
And all my roses; yet in spite of you,

There is one crown I bear away with me,
And to-night, when I enter before God,
My salute shall sweep all the stars away
From the blue threshold! One thing without stain,
Unspotted from the world, in spite of doom
Mine own!—
(*He springs forward, his sword aloft*)
        And that is . . .
(*The sword escapes from his hand; he totters, and falls into the arms of* LE BRET *and* RAGUENEAU)

ROXANE (*bends over him and kisses him on the forehead*):
                —That is . . .

CYRANO (*opens his eyes and smiles up at her*):
                   My white plume. . . .

CURTAIN